Lekha Publishers LLC.

D0771758

The Sassy Divas

Yalda Alexandra Saii

Text Copyright © 2012 Yalda Alexandra Saii
Cover Design and Interior Design by Novella Genelza
Editor-in-Chief: Novella Genelza
Editors: Carter Jung, Jyoti Yelagalawadi, Keith White, and Katie May

Typset in Jenna Sue, Kittyspoon, Angelina, SweetiePie, Wellbutrin, and Book
Antiqua

All rights reserved. No part of this publication may be reproduced or transmitted
in any form or by any means, electronic or mechanical, including photography,
recording, or any information storage and retrieval system now known or to be
invented, without permission in writing from the publisher, except by a reviewer
who wishes to quote brief passages in connection with a review written for
inclusion in a magazine, newspaper, or broadcast.

ISBN: 978-1-937675-08-0

Published in the United States by:
Lekha Publishers LLC.
4204 Latimer Avenue, San Jose, CA 95130
www.LekhaInk.com

Acknowledgements

When I was younger I loved reading books about popular girls. It was a fascinating subject to me. Those books played an active role in my decision to start writing *The Sassy Divas*, along with my own personal experiences growing up. Middle school can be a tough time for most kids, and themes like friendship and the drama that sometimes comes with it were easy for me to write about. I wanted to write a book which readers my age could enjoy and relate to.

I would like to thank my friends and family, especially my wonderful parents. Thanks to their love and encouragement, I have been able to follow my dreams and become a published author.

I am also very grateful to the publishing and teaching staff at Lekha, including my teacher Katie May. Thank you all for your support and dedication. The journey to get this book finished and published was tedious but very exciting at the same time, and there were many bumps in the road. There were some frustrating times when I felt like discarding what I had written of *The Sassy Divas* and just moving on to something else, but I was always told not to give up on it. Now, looking back, I am so glad that I didn't.

I am also very thankful to my peers in my advanced writing class at Lekha. Their feedback during our work-shopping sessions was very helpful during the editing process. They pointed out the good and the bad in my rough drafts and gave me valuable comments that really helped me with my rewrites. Not only did they help me improve *The Sassy Divas*, but their excitement about my novel made me excited as well.

Lastly, thank you—the reader. It means so much to me to be able to share this novel with you.

-Yalda Alexandra Saii

Chapter One

It was a rainy day at Peckerson Middle School. Raindrops splattered hard against the windows, and the shiny silver doorknobs on the dark blue doors were cold. It was morning break, but we were stuck inside our homeroom due to the rain. I was in the back of the room talking with the other girls in my clique — the Sassy Divas. I, Vanessa Pocker, was the leader. I had straight blonde hair that was as soft as feathers and fell just past my shoulders. Long, dark brown eyelashes framed my bright blue eyes. Adrienne and Chelsea were pretty as well, but not as pretty as me. Adrienne had long, light brown waves and dark brown eyes. Katie had long, red hair and brown eyes, and her face was dusted with light freckles. Chelsea had the most unique look out of all of us—she had chin-length, dark auburn hair with bangs and emerald green eyes.

"I can't believe we're stuck indoors!" Adrienne groaned, eyeing our other classmates with disgust.

"It's okay, Adrienne," I said. "We'll be able to go outside another day."

"But I really want to go outside today!" Chelsea whined.

"I hate rain..." Katie murmured.

"We'll go outside tomorrow!" I hissed.

The girls instantly went quiet. They knew they shouldn't whine like that. I heard some bookworms groan. I frowned. The Sassy Divas were awesome. We were the most popular girls in the school, whether they liked it or not. I was the Ruler of the School, if you will. We started out as just a group of pretty fashionistas, but then we started setting trends. That's when we really got noticed. Quickly, we became the trendsetters of the school. Besides being extremely fashionable, we were also known for being sassy, and of course, divas. What great fashion icon wouldn't be? The name sort of stuck, and we started calling ourselves the Sassy Divas too. In addition to being the most popular girls in school, we were some of the richest too. Even though Peckerson was a public school, it was near the coast of Santa Monica, one of the trendiest and most affluent areas of Los Angeles. So most of the students had big allowances, but ours were bigger. Being the richest was always better because you got the coolest designer clothes and the thinnest new laptops as soon as they hit the stores.

"Students," announced our homeroom teacher, Mrs. Putt. "Break is over. You're going to have to go to your next class now." We shuffled over to science class. Our science teacher, Mr. Lyons, told us to work quietly on our science workbooks while he graded papers. But I wanted to do something else. I took out a sheet of notepaper while Mr. Lyons was in the back of the room, and started making notes about the Sassy Divas for the members, just in case they had forgotten some of our most important rules. And considering how annoying they had been lately… maybe some of them had.

Sassy Divas Rules

What The Sassy Divas Do:
Gossip
Have fun
Shop
Talk
Set Trends
Donate $30 a month to the S.D. bank account

What The Sassy Divas DON'T Do:
Disrespect Vanessa
Disobey Vanessa
Annoy Vanessa
Dress badly
Act nerdy
Care about school (but we still do homework)

Members:
Me (Vanessa)
Katie
Adrienne
Chelsea

Who You're Not Allowed to Talk to and Why:
Jenn (refused to give me a pen)
Florence (refused to hold my purse)
Owen (stepped on my foot)

I was admiring my list when I was interrupted by my best friend, Katie. "What are you gonna do after school, V?" she whispered.

"I'm gonna do *stuff*," I hissed back. It was none of her business what I was planning on doing! "What about you?"

"Um... I might go hang out at somebody's house..."

I looked at her suspiciously. I wondered who she was planning to see. "Okay..."

Before I could ask Katie more questions, Mr. Lyons clapped his hands together enthusiastically. He placed a stack of papers on his desk and went to the whiteboard. "Lecture time!" he announced.

Katie took out her science notebook and a pen. I craned my neck so I could read over her shoulder as she flipped through the pages. I noticed that she had loose pieces of paper filled with problems and notes. Was she *actually* taking extra notes and practicing her math at home? Sassy Divas *do not* do extra work. As I was thinking about this, a sticky note fell out of her notebook. Nerdy Katie was so busy taking notes that she didn't notice it. It landed next to my desk. I quickly scooped it up. Florence's Email address was scribbled across it. In the *Sassy Divas Rules*, Florence was under "Who You're Not Allowed to Talk to and Why." I crumpled the sticky note into a tiny ball and stuffed it into my pocket. Was it Florence that she was going to see after school?

✩ ✩ ✩

When I got home, my mom was in the kitchen preparing dinner. "How was school, honey?" she asked, glancing up from the pile of vegetables she was chopping. My mom loved cooking. She said it took her mind off of all the stress she had to deal with, working as a lawyer.

"You know, the usual," I answered, searching our bright white cabinets for a snack. I unwrapped a chewy chocolate chip granola bar, and took a bite. *Mmmm!* Chewy bars always hit the spot after school. I leaned against the counter, savoring each mouthful.

"Okay, if you say so. How's Ryan? Was he at school today?" Ryan was my best guy friend. He wasn't bad-looking, with his slightly wavy, dark brown hair that fell just a little bit over his light green eyes, but we were strictly friends. I could trust him with anything.

"Uh, yeah, he was there, but I didn't talk to him. He's *a guy*, Mom, so my Divas and I don't really socialize with him at school. The Divas are a girls-only clique. Duh."

"That's too bad. Do you have any homework?"

"Yeah. Not that much, though."

"Great! Well make sure to finish your work fast so you can watch TV with me! I just recorded a new episode of that cool show about people with weird addictions…" my mom said, smiling excitedly.

"Oh… wait! I just remembered that we actually *do* have a lot of homework tonight. There's some extra assignments due soon!" I interrupted quickly. "Sorry, I guess that means I can't watch that weird show with you! *Bummer!*"

I hated that show. My mom loved it.

I finished my bar and walked upstairs to my room. I decided to call Katie to see what she was up to. I punched in her number and flopped down onto my perfectly made, pale lavender bed.

"Hello?"

"Hey Katie," I said.

"Oh! Vanessa! Hi!" Katie said.

"Where are you?"

"Does it matter?"

I widened my eyes. *Did she seriously just say that?* "Does it matter? Does it matter?!" I shouted angrily. "Yes, it *does* matter! Where are you?"

"At a friend's house."

"Oh, that friend you were talking about today at school?"

"Er... yeah..."

Silence.

"Listen, V. I have to go." Katie hung up.

"Why, is *Florence* waiting?" I screeched. I felt like throwing my cell phone, but I didn't want to ruin the brand new glitter case I had just bought for it. So I put it on my desk and began to punch my pillow. I punched it over and over and over, until my mom called me down for dinner.

After a delicious dinner of pesto pasta, I told my mom I was going to go to bed. I brushed my teeth, washed my face, changed into my pajamas, and got under the covers. I always tried to think of happy stuff to help myself fall asleep, like shopping or being crowned Prom Queen someday. That night, I tried so hard to think pleasant thoughts, but I could only think of Katie. Had she forgotten the three most important rules in the *Sassy Divas Rules*? Don't disrespect, disobey, or annoy Vanessa. She was doing all three! I had to remind Katie who was boss. I had to get her back under my control!

Let's see... I thought. *Maybe I should buy something really cute for Katie. She'll love it so much that she'll remember how awesome I am, and how she would never want to leave me! Then she'll obey me! And she'll stop disrespecting and annoying me! It's brilliant! Tomorrow I'll*

wake up really early and stop by the beauty store on the way to school. I'll get her that trendy nail polish and glittery eyeliner she wanted! Oh my gosh, I'm the smartest girl ever!

It was a fantastic idea.

Chapter Two

"Miss Pocker, you will be serving Study Hall again tomorrow…" our math teacher, Mr. Ton, grumbled. The Bookworms giggled. I sighed. I waited with the rest of the class as Mr. Ton read off the names of the rest of the people who were going to serve Study Hall. "…Matt, Adam, Thomas, Chelsea, and last but not least, Adrienne," he finished with a sarcastic smile. "Okay, everyone. Let's begin by going over last night's homework."

Katie didn't get Study Hall? I thought. *The Sassy Divas always get Study Hall! We don't study! We do as little work as possible! In fact, Katie hadn't gotten Study Hall in a long time… and on the day before the history test a week ago, when I video chatted with Katie, I could see her history textbook and notebook lying on the ground. Was she actually studying? And did she really care about school?*

I looked at Katie. She took out her white binder. When she opened it, I noticed that there were photo booth pictures in one of the clear side pockets. The pictures were of her and a girl with shoulder-length, curly dark brown hair. The girl looked like Florence.

At lunch, Adrienne, Chelsea, and I sat down at our table. Adrienne and Chelsea were gossiping excitedly about their latest celebrity crushes. I was the first one to notice that Katie wasn't with us.

"Wait a second… where's Katie?" I glared at the other two girls.

Chelsea shrugged. "Don't know. She's been acting kinda different lately."

"I'm going to go find her," I sighed, getting up.

The first place I checked was her locker. She wasn't there. After roaming the halls a while, I had to go to the bathroom. As soon as I locked the stall door, I heard the door swing open. I heard Katie's voice say, "Make sure no else is in here." My eyes widened. I closed the toilet seat slowly and carefully stepped onto it, trying to be as quiet as possible. It was hard since the soles of my boots kept slipping on the dirty toilet seat lid.

I heard footsteps. Katie and the other girl were checking to see if they could see feet below the stalls. I held my breath as they passed my stall.

"No one's in here, Katie. What do you want to tell me?"

Katie sighed. "I think Vanessa knows something's up, Florence." I gaped.

"So? I thought you were my friend!" Florence said.

"I am. I like you a lot. You're a great friend, Flo, but I... I still like Vanessa too. And she doesn't like you. At all."

"Okay...?"

"And, if I'm BFF with you, then I can't be BFF with Vanessa. So... we can't hang out at school anymore. But we can still be BFF."

"Um..."

"Sorry, Flo. If she sees me with you... I won't be allowed to be in The Sassy Divas anymore."

"But you're honestly not even a real Sassy Diva—" *Not a real Sassy Diva?! What was that supposed to mean?*

"Florence!" Katie cut her off.

Florence sighed. "Fine. Do what you want." There was an awkward silence, then Florence stomped out of the restroom, slamming the door behind her. Then I heard some weird sniffling sounds, like Katie was actually crying or something! *How stupid. This was all Florence's fault.*

The sniffling stopped. I carefully peeked through the crack in the stall door, to see what Katie was doing. She turned on the faucet and yanked some paper towels from the roll, wet them, and wiped the tears from her face before leaving the restroom.

For at least a minute after she left, I couldn't move. My mouth was still open. I was in shock. *How could Katie have betrayed me like this?* I felt like screaming, but I was in the restroom—the sound would surely ring through the halls. Instead, I burst out of the stall and turned on the sink. I wet my hands, pumping a bunch of soap and lathering it all up. Then I ran around the bathroom, flinging the suds all over the place angrily.

"I... hate... FLORENCE!" I exclaimed, flinging the suds even harder.

I flushed every toilet in the restroom with my soapy hands. I pulled the toilet paper in every stall.

Afterwards, I took a deep breath, rinsed and dried my hands, carefully smoothed my hair, reapplied my lipgloss, and walked confidently out of the restroom.

After school, I decided to go to Sugar Cafe by myself. Sugar Cafe was my favorite after-school spot, and it was just a short walk away from campus. I wanted coffee and a cake pop. Plus I needed to think things through. As I walked along the pretty, tree-lined path that led to Sugar Cafe, I couldn't stop thinking about the secret conversation between Katie and Flo. I couldn't believe they were BFF now. Katie was supposed to be *my* best friend. There was no way I would let her stay best friends with Florence. Friends don't let friends befriend losers.

The wind blew my hair, which bothered me because it made my hair messy. My hair was not supposed to be messy. Even though nobody else was around, I flattened it quickly. I looked around again to make sure I was really alone. There was nothing but a row of trees on either side of me. The leaves were gold, my favorite color. With every step I took, the leaves crunched satisfyingly beneath my sand-colored Uggs.

Suddenly, the rhythmic crunching of the leaves was messed up by the sound of another pair of feet, moving much faster than mine. "Hey!" yelled a voice behind me. "Vanessa!" As I turned around, my glossy blonde hair swished from one shoulder to the other. It was Katie. She was running towards me. "Wait up!"

I waited until she caught up. When she reached me, she ran her fingers through her long, red hair, smoothing it. She smiled at me sweetly. I didn't smile back. "What are you doing here?" I asked, starting to walk again, moving quicker this time.

Katie hurried to keep up with me. "I'm going to Sugar Cafe to get tea." she said.

"Tea? Hmm… not coffee?"

"Yeah. Tea. Coffee's gross."

"Nobody asked you!" I snapped.

Katie frowned. We kept walking. After a few minutes, she decided to break the silence. "Mr. Ton is *so* annoying," she said. "We have so much math homework. I don't think I can video chat tonight." I didn't reply.

About a minute later, we reached Sugar Cafe. We stepped inside, and a musical door chime announced our arrival. I smiled as I inhaled the scent of sweet mocha and sugary pastries. The walls were painted pink and covered with pictures of tea, cookies, and cake. The floor was bright, tan-colored wood. The chairs and tables were white with light pink hearts in the middle. It was an adorable place. The only thing that bothered me was the owners, Mr. and Mrs. Harris. They were super jolly, which was so annoying. Katie loved them.

"Good afternoon, cuties!" Mrs. Harris greeted us cheerfully as we walked in. She had a big smile on her face. I fake-smiled and waved. Mrs. Harris turned back to her customers. Katie and I sat down at a nearby table. While Katie filed her nails, I looked over at Mrs. Harris. She had pale pink lipstick on, the color of strawberry cupcakes, and blue eyes. She was wearing a white apron covered in ruffles. Her light gray hair was tied up in a high bun. "Can you order for us?" Katie asked me, examining her manicure.

"No," I replied flatly. Katie sighed and got up.

"I want a small coffee and a tiramisu cake pop," I added, as she headed towards the cash register.

After buying everything, Katie sat back down next to me. I took a gulp of my coffee and proceeded to eat my cake pop in silence. Katie sipped her mint tea awkwardly.

"So, Katie," I swallowed the last bit of my cake pop. "Lunch. You weren't with us."

Katie looked at me blankly and then let out a tiny, nervous laugh. "Oh, right. I wasn't, huh?"

"Well, where were you?"

"Er... at my locker." Katie said, quickly.

"No, you weren't. I checked." I replied, with raised eyebrows.

"I was at my locker for only a bit," Katie said. "Then I went... um... to the bathroom."

"Why?"

Katie looked at me, doubtfully. "Well, I had to pee..."

"Okay, um, what I meant was, did you take anyone with you?"

Katie blinked and then grinned widely. "Haha! Who would I take with me?"

"Oh, I don't know. Florence, maybe?"

Katie turned pale for a moment, then shrugged it off. "Heh. Well, no, I went by myself."

"Of course you did." I gave Katie a knowing look.

Katie quickly took a sip of mint tea, keeping her eyes locked on her cup.

"But anyway," I continued. I was determined to get the truth out of her. "What's up with Florence? You guys seem kind of close all of a sudden."

"Oh, no. Of course not. I *hate* Florence, V. She's so... nerdy. She called the other night to ask me a random Harry Potter question. Like, outta the blue."

"Why would she choose to ask *you* that, out of everyone at school?"

"Beats me," Katie took another sip of tea. "Maybe I look like the Harry Potter type."

"Whatevs. *I'm so Team Twilight.*"

Katie shrugged.

"Aren't you *Team Twilight* too?" I asked. "Because last time I checked, you've never even read *Harry Potter*."

"Of course I haven't!" Katie laughed nervously. "I've never, ever read it. Not even once. I'm so totally

Team Twilight! Anyway, Florence is a total nerd. Hate her."

"If you hate her, then why were you talking to her secretly in the restroom at lunch?"

"What? I did not!"

"Katie, I'm not an idiot."

Katie's eyes started getting glassy. "Okay, fine! I *did* talk to Florence in the restroom at lunch! I love Florence! She's so fun and nice! We're, like, BFF! But, V, I love you too! I love the Sassy Divas and it's a complete honor to be in your clique, but I still like Flo a ton! I'm sorry, V, I really am!" Tears began to roll slowly down Katie's cheeks.

"Well, Katie, that doesn't solve anything. I'm afraid I have to kick you out of the Sassy Divas."

"What?" Katie dabbed at her tears with a pink paper napkin.

"You... are... out... of.... the... Sassy... Divas," I said slowly. I felt like I was communicating with someone from a different country.

"Just for hanging out with Flo?" Katie said angrily.

"Yep. You've been pretty different lately. I don't want to deal with that."

Katie got up. "You know what, Vanessa? You are the most controlling *dog* I've ever met!"

"What happened to loving me?"

"I changed my mind," Katie replied, fluffing her bangs.

"Okay, whatevs."

"And apparently you don't have any feelings!"

"And apparently you don't have any brain," I responded casually.

"I'm obviously smarter than you, so I have no clue what you're talking about!" Katie yelled.

"Girls!" Mrs. Harris scolded loudly. We ignored her.

"Anyone smarter than me is a nerd!" I yelled in Katie's face.

"Ugh!" Katie threw her tea at me.

I gasped, disgusted. I looked down. My outfit was stained with warm mint tea. It felt as if I had peed myself. I screamed. Loudly.

Now, everybody was looking at us.

"*Girls!*" Mrs. Harris yelled loudly. She pointed at the door. "*Get out.*"

I ran out. Katie followed.

"Wait, Vanessa, I—" Katie called after me.

"Shut up and get lost, Katie!" I screamed, without looking back. I didn't stop running until I got home. I ran up to my room and locked the door.

☆ ☆ ☆

I lay on my bed, sulking for hours. My mom kept knocking on my door, trying to get me to come downstairs to eat. I told her I wasn't hungry. *Why wouldn't everyone just leave me alone?* I took out my frustration on my pillows again, punching them and throwing them against every wall, until my room was a hopeless mess. My rhinestone-covered pencil holder was knocked over on my desk, and all my gel pens had spilled out over my white laptop's keyboard. The adorable cashmere cardigan I had draped over my rolling chair now lay on my fluffy white carpet. The poster I got from a fashion show I went to in New York was now hanging on only one pushpin, slowly swaying. Looking around, I sighed. Exhausted, I dozed off. I was woken up by a video chat request from Adrienne and Chelsea. I accepted it.

"Hey Vanessa! How's it going?" Adrienne and Chelsea grinned.

"Hey girls…" I mumbled in a low voice.

"Whoa. V. You sound really sad. What's wrong?" Chelsea asked. I straightened up.

"Nothing. Listen, girls, you're not allowed to talk to Katie. She's out of the Sassy Divas."

The girls gasped.

"Why?" Adrienne asked.

"I think she's a secret Bookworm," I said. "She was being really rude to me today. Plus, she's best friends with Florence... that loser."

"Oh... that's not good," Adrienne said, shaking her head sympathetically.

"So... yeah..." I said, looking down. "I don't really feel like chatting right now."

"That's cool," Chelsea assured me with a soft smile. "We totally understand."

"Yeah," Adrienne agreed.

"Thanks, you guys," I gave them my best attempt at a smile. "Bye." I left the video chat and immediately called Ryan.

"What's up, V?" he answered cheerfully.

"Major drama, Ryan."

"What is it?"

"Well, uh, Katie just got kicked out of the Sassy Divas." I could practically see Ryan rolling his eyes on the other end of the line. He hated the idea of the Sassy Divas, but he still supported me because he was a great friend. We had been friends since kindergarten, way before I had even met any of the Divas.

"I'm sorry to hear that. But you guys can still be friends, right?"

I let out an exasperated sigh. "Ryan, don't you know *anything*? She's *kicked out* of The Sassy Divas. The Sassy Divas are my group of friends. Duh!"

"But why did you kick her out?"

"She's turned into a Bookworm. Gross, right?"

"I guess... but Katie's so nice!"

I laughed. "Uh, no! She was being so disobedient. I'm sick of her."

"So then you guys aren't friends at all anymore?"

"That's what I just said, Ryan!"

"Right. Sorry about you losing Katie."

"Oh, don't worry about it. I'm so over it. It happened, like, a while ago."

"Oh! Why didn't you tell me earlier?"

"Well... it happened at school today..."

"So, why'd you call me then if you're over it?"

"I... uh..." I sighed. "Fine, okay? I'm not over it. I mean, I still really like Katie, but I just can't have her as my friend anymore!"

"Why not?"

"It's complicated and kind of hard to explain, but basically I have to let her go for the sake of my image. Katie has chosen the way of the Bookworm. I can't have a Bookworm in the Sassy Divas."

"Why not?" Ryan asked. He was so clueless. I let out another exasperated sigh.

"Because, Ryan, I'm a Sassy Diva and Bookworms are... well.... *Bookworms!* They're always reading and acting nerdy and they don't like shopping and other fun stuff."

"But weren't *you* a Bookworm once?"

I froze, remembering the beginning of sixth grade. It was before I transferred to Peckerson Middle School. I flashed back to memories of the constant teasing, the parties I wasn't invited to, the Autumn mixer I went to by myself, wearing a hideously embarrassing dress...

"We are *not* talking about that, Ryan! The past is the past!" I snapped quickly.

There was another awkward pause. "Well, V, what's meant to be will always find its way, right?"

I had no idea what he was talking about. Ryan was always trying to sound so deep and smart. "I guess..." I trailed off.

"Well, I have to go now. I have soccer practice." Ryan said, filling the silence. "Catch you later, V."

"Later, Ryan." I hung up.

Chapter Three

The Sassy Divas were telling me that I should find another person to join our clique. "It just feels kind of *empty* without Katie," Chelsea murmured.

I glared at Chelsea. "It does not." Chelsea looked down.

"I really want to go make fun of her," Adrienne said.

"Ohmygosh, such a good idea!" I grinned. "Okay, let's see... there she is! Right over there! She's eating with the Bookworms!"

The Divas and I walked towards Katie. She was sitting at a table with her Bookworm friends. When we stood in front of her, a few Bookworms glanced at us, but then they continued chatting with Katie.

I cleared my throat. Katie didn't look at me. Neither did anyone else. "Hi Katie," I said. "You're looking very cute today in Mrs. Putt's skirt." Chelsea and Adrienne snickered. Mrs. Putt always wore the ugliest clothes out of all the teachers at Peckerson Middle School.

Katie ignored me. Adrienne looked at me seriously. "Oh, Vanessa. We forgot. She only speaks Dog," she said. I tried hard not to laugh. "Here, let me try to talk to her." Adrienne looked at Katie. She looked as if she was concentrating. Then she said, "Ruff, ruff, ruff, ruff, ruff! Ruff! Ruff, ruff!"

Katie rolled her eyes at Adrienne. Then she replied, "Ruff, ruff, ruff, ruff! Ruff, ruff!" Florence gave her a slightly confused look.

"Ruff, ruff, ruff, ruff!" Chelsea joined in.

"Ruff, ruff!" I cried.

We looked like idiots. Katie, Adrienne, Chelsea, and I, speaking Dog to each other, even though we weren't even supposed to be friends with Katie.

"Ruff, ruff, ruff, ruff, *ruff!*" Katie shouted back, hiding a small smile.

"Okay, that's *enough!*" I said, finally putting an end to it. Nobody made a sound. "Katie," I said, looking straight into her eyes. "Mrs. Putt wants her skirt back."

The Sassy Divas and I left, cracking up.

✫ ✫ ✫

The next day, during math class, we got our tests back.

"And the person with the highest score on the test is... Katie!" Mr. Ton announced. "She got a one-hundred percent."

Of course. Katie got a one-hundred percent on her math test. Now she had to give a speech, which would probably be *beyond* boring.

Katie walked to the front of the class and bowed. "Wow... I'm so happy! I never thought this moment would come..." Katie grinned a stupid grin. It's not like she was winning a Grammy! "I really want to thank all my friends in the Homework Buddies Club! I don't think I've ever gotten the highest score on a test before!"

The Homework Buddies Club? I rolled my eyes as the Bookworms gave Katie a standing ovation.

"Well, Katie, you're a very smart girl," Mr. Ton said as he returned to the whiteboard to continue the day's lesson. "Congratulations."

I got up and went to sanitize my hands in the back of the room.

Later, during computer class, Katie got another standing ovation from the Bookworms when we had to take a typing test. Katie typed ninety-five words per minute, and Miss Anderson was very proud.

"Great work, Katie!" she grinned.

"Thank you," Katie blushed.

Show-off.

✿ ✿ ✿

At lunch, Katie sat with the Bookworms. I walked up to her. "Katie," I said.

Katie did not reply.

I cleared my throat.

Katie did not look up.

"Katie."

Katie still didn't say or do anything.

Great. Now she was ignoring me. I exhaled loudly and walked away, murmuring, "Whatever."

"V?" Adrienne said softly, as I sat back down at the Sassy Divas' usual lunch table.

"What?" I asked, tucking a strand of hair behind my ears.

"Is everything okay?"

"Yes, Adrienne, everything is *fine.*" I snapped. I wasn't in the mood for conversation.

"Okay." Adrienne went back to quietly eating her sandwich. I pushed my food around my plate until the bell rang.

Everything *wasn't* fine. Katie was ignoring me, she was a Teacher's Pet, and she was the newest member of the Homework Buddies Club, a nerdy club that did homework and extra credit together after school. It seemed like Katie was going her own way, and she didn't want me anymore. Whatever. I didn't want her either.

☆ ☆ ☆

That weekend, the Sassy Divas and I made plans to go to the mall. My mom said she'd drive us. The first stop was Adrienne's. She was already on her porch, sitting on a pale green bench and reading *Seventeen* magazine. The window behind her was open, and I could see her mom inside washing dishes. My mom honked her horn. Adrienne looked up from *Seventeen* and smiled. She stuffed her magazine into her purse, shouted goodbye to her mom, and ran to our car. She opened the back passenger door, and hopped in next to me.

"Hi Adrienne!" my mom said, cheerfully.

"Hey, Mrs. Pocker!" Adrienne replied. Then she turned to me. "So, I was reading *Seventeen*…"

As Adrienne filled me in on the latest trends and celebrity gossip, my mom reached Katie's house. *Crud. I had forgotten to tell her.* Katie was on her lawn with her cousin, Brianna. They were having a picnic. Katie stared at Adrienne and I, wide-eyed with surprise. Adrienne and I hushed up and glared back. Brianna turned to look at us too. We stared back. Talk about an awkward moment.

"Is Brianna coming too, Vanessa?" My mom asked.

"Um… Actually, Katie and Brianna had other plans today," Adrienne offered quickly.

"Yeah," I agreed, relieved by Adrienne's quick thinking. "Sorry I forgot to tell you, Mom!"

My mom looked at me for a minute in the rear-view mirror. Her eyebrows were raised and it looked like she was going to say something. Then she just sighed and drove off towards Chelsea's house.

☆ ☆ ☆

When we got home from the mall, I decided to play *Doodle Jump* on my cell phone. Then the home phone rang. My mom picked it up. "Hello?" I heard her answer from downstairs. "Oh, Katie! Hi!"

I jumped off my bed and ran to pick up the phone in the study so I could listen in on their conversation.

"I'm great, thank you!" my mom said. "How are you?"

"I'm good! So, I hear that the stock market's been going up!" *Nerd.*

"Oh yes! Delightful, isn't it?"

"Yes, very!" Katie replied eagerly.

"It's a shame that you couldn't make it to go shopping at the mall today with Vanessa, Adrienne, and Chelsea," my mom said, changing the subject. Katie was silent for a few seconds, but then she seemed to figure out the situation.

"Yes," she said. "As you saw, I was with my cousin, Brianna."

"Well, spending quality time with family is always a good thing."

"Yes… um, Mrs. Pocker? May I please speak with Vanessa now?"

"Certainly!"

My eyes widened.

"Vanessa! Phone's for you!" my mom yelled.

I purposefully waited for a few seconds, so they wouldn't suspect that I had been listening in.

"Got it!" I yelled back. My mom hung up. Katie didn't say anything. "Hello, you have reached the

Pocker Residence," I said, using my best fake British accent. "May I ask who is speaking?"

"It's Katie."

"What do you want?" I snapped.

"Why didn't you tell your mother that we're not friends anymore?"

"Um, it's none of your business!"

Katie sighed.

"Why did you call?" I demanded.

"I just wanted to let you know that you should really tell her, because every time you and your Sassy Divas go somewhere, I don't want your mother to just drive up to my house."

"Yeah, I guess I don't want that either."

"Exactly."

"Okay, I'll let her know. I don't want you to ever call me again, by the way," I said, slamming the phone back into its holder.

Chapter Four

"Darlings," Miss Rayne said the next day. "Take out a sheet of paper, and please begin drawing a calm scene. A scene that would make people smile, close their eyes, and dream..." Miss Rayne was our hippie art teacher.

I thought for a moment, imagining calm places. The makeup store makes *me* dream, that's for sure. And designer clothing boutiques... but something told me those weren't the kind of scenes that Miss Rayne meant. Then I immediately thought of something else. The spa. The spa was so much more amazing than some crummy nature scene. As soon as I began sketching, the door swung open, and a new girl popped in.

Her hair was straight, chest-length, and light brown, and her dark green eyes weren't hideous, but the rest of the package was! Big, peachy-colored frames hid her pretty eyes, and her outfit... oh, her outfit! She was wearing a loose white t-shirt printed with the logo of some event at her local library, and plain black yoga pants. Her shoes were boring white tennis shoes from Target. And lastly, she had silver braces. Don't get me wrong—there's nothing much you can do about braces. After all, their purpose is to make your teeth perfect! But they are definitely not the perfect fashion accessory. I am so glad that I was born with straight teeth.

Her whole look reminded me of myself two years before. It was terrible. I always tried to block those memories from my head, but I could never get rid of them completely. My hair, which was so straight and soft now, used to be coarse and messy. My outfits, which were now trendy designer brands, used to be just plain t-shirts and unflattering jeans. And my face used to be covered in little pink zits... I shook my head to get the awful thoughts out of my mind. "She looks *horrible*," I whispered to my Divas.

"Hi guys! I'm Quinn Daphne Richardson, and I'm shadowing today!" the girl announced happily, clutching her metal sandwich lunchbox (you know, those ones that are actually shaped like sandwiches).

"Crud! She just *had* to come during second period to ruin my day!" I hissed at my fellow Sassy Divas, who were sitting next to me, of course. "She could have at least come during fifth period!"

"I know, right?" Adrienne whispered back.

"Agreed," Chelsea hissed. "Look at her shirt... how gross!"

"Oh, how wonderful," Miss Rayne beamed at the new girl. "Please take a seat at one of the tables... you can put your lunchbox in the back... and get a piece of paper from the table and start drawing a calm scene."

"Okay!" Quinn grinned. She put her things away, grabbed a piece of paper, then decided to sit down... at Katie's table.

"Quinn!" Katie smiled. "I'm Katie." Katie pointed to Florence. "This is Florence."

"Hi Florence," Quinn smiled.

"Hi Quinn," Florence grinned back.

"Is it okay if I sit here?" Quinn asked.

"Of course!" Katie smiled.

I tried to ignore them and continued drawing my spa scene, putting extra pressure on my pencil. *I never had any friends when I looked like Quinn.* I snuck a few glances at them as I sketched. Every five minutes or so, they would all burst into laughter. It seemed like they were having a lot of fun. I was sure that what they were talking about wasn't really that funny, and that Katie probably just told them to laugh loudly to get my attention. That's the kind of thing Katie would do. I knew she still had a little bit of Sassy Diva in her.

"You guys are so cool," Quinn grinned.

"Thanks!" Florence grinned.

"You're cool, too," Katie said sincerely.

"Do you mind if I sit with you at lunch?"

"Of course not!" Florence said.

Katie and Quinn were becoming friends? No. No! NO! There was no way I would let Katie get *another* new friend. I had to get revenge. Thus began my plan: steal Quinn from Katie.

Later that day, while I walked home, I called Ryan on my cell. I had to rant to someone, and he was always the perfect person to rant to.

"Ryan!"

"Vanessa!" Ryan mimicked.

"You won't *believe* what happened today!" I exclaimed.

"You bought an adorable new top?"

I cracked a small smile. "No, Ryan, I didn't, unfortunately. That would've really brightened my day."

"Then what happened?"

"There was a new girl shadowing at school today."

"I know, Vanessa. I go to your school."

"Well, that new girl is a total *nerd*," I said, dismissing his smart remark.

"So...?"

I rolled my eyes. "So, she wants to hang out with the Bookworms. Guess who's a Bookworm? Katie is a Bookworm. Today, Quinn — the nerd — sat with Katie and Florence during Art. They laughed and had a good time and now they're becoming friends and that *can't happen!*"

"And why not?"

"Because, Ryan, then Katie and Florence are going to have a new friend and a new member of their little posse! That just can't happen! Katie is supposed to learn that without me, she can't even have a good time and make new friends! But what is she doing? MAKING NEW FRIENDS! UGH!" I yelled.

"Oh...?" He clearly wasn't getting it.

"Oh?! You're not even comforting me! Why not?! You're supposed to comfort me! You're my best guy friend! And guy friends are supposed to help their girl friends when their girl friends have girl problems!"

"Sorry, sorry! Everything will be alright, Vanessa! Just follow your heart and —"

"I just have to get Quinn away from Katie!" I snapped.

"How are you going to do that?"

"I'll find a way!"

"Alright then..." he muttered. There went that imaginary eye-roll again. I sighed as I stepped into my house.

"Gotta go now, Ryan. I just got home. See you around." I hung up.

Chapter Five

"I seriously hope Quinn *hates* this school and decides not to come here!" I told Adrienne and Chelsea the next day before school.

"Totally…" Chelsea agreed.

"But it's possible that she actually *transferred* here yesterday after school! How depressing is that?!" Adrienne complained.

"Very!" Chelsea replied.

"Oh, crud," I said, frozen.

"What?" Adrienne asked, worried. She grabbed my hand.

"She's back," Chelsea whispered.

Quinn had just stepped out of a blue Volvo and was walking towards the school. I could tell by Adrienne's facial expression that she was cussing in her head. I didn't blame her. "What are we going to do?" Chelsea whispered with a panicked expression.

"Girls!" I hissed. "We have to deal with this. We are Sassy Divas, after all, *not* six year-olds!"

Chelsea and Adrienne straightened up, and I knew they were ready to fight.

I looked over at Quinn to see where she had gone. She was next to Katie. I coughed loudly several times to get the Divas' attention.

"Yes?" Chelsea asked, looking at me. When I didn't say anything, she followed my eyes. She narrowed her eyes at Quinn.

Adrienne did the same.

"Girls?" I said.

"Yeah?" Chelsea and Adrienne said.

"We have to act. *Now*."

☆ ☆ ☆

Finally, it was lunch. The most important time of the school day. After grabbing our lunch boxes, we headed to the field behind the school. It was pretty deserted at lunchtime, so we knew nobody would see us. Our plan was to butter Quinn up. If she hung out with us, she'd be stop hanging out with Katie. That way, Quinn wouldn't influence Katie, and make her into even more of a loser than she was already becoming. After that, I would find a way to get Katie back. Nerds are gullible. I knew what I was doing.

Adrienne and I took a seat on the grass, while Chelsea went to the bathroom to change into a disguise. Since we didn't want to be seen asking a major loser to sit with us, Chelsea went to the bathroom and threw on a long Gucci trench coat and some huge Fendi shades with dark lenses. Then she walked over to the lunch area where Quinn was sitting, and asked her to come to the field to "sit with that girl from art class." Quinn followed her order loyally, and sat down on the grass with us.

"Wait! You two are those popular girls!" she gasped, with wide eyes. Then she turned to Chelsea, who had just taken off her glasses and coat. "So *you* were the one wearing the detective coat?"

"Detective coat? DETECTIVE COAT?!" Chelsea yelled. "This is a GUCCI TRENCH COAT! How *dare* you call it a detective coat!"

Quinn slumped. "Oh, I'm sorry…"

"You should be!" Chelsea chided.

Adrienne kicked Chelsea's foot. Chelsea winced and shut up.

"So, Quinn!" I grinned, flashing a bright smile. "Tell us about yourself!"

"Okay! Well, I love going to school and my pet frog, Equation!" she beamed.

Equation the Frog? I thought. *Ridiculous*. "How, um… cute…" I forced myself to reply.

"I'm also a BIG FAN of watching Spongebob!" she added, happily unaware of how much she was boring me. "And my favorite color is denim. Denim is such a pretty shade of blue…"

"How about your favorite pop singer?" Adrienne interrupted, desperate for the tiniest bit of interesting information. "Jason Lovel is *my* absolute favorite. He's so dreamy…" she added, smiling wistfully.

"Um… well, I'm not really a big music person…" Quinn stammered.

"You mean you don't even have a favorite song?" Adrienne asked, with eyebrows raised.

"Oh, of course I do! My favorite song is 'Symphony Five' by Beethoven."

Chelsea and I chuckled. Adrienne rolled her eyes.

"I've only sat here for a few minutes, but you guys seem super cool!" Quinn squealed.

The Divas and I laughed.

After lunch, on our way to class, we passed Katie and the Bookworms in the hallway. I looked at Katie. She looked back at me. For a moment, my blue eyes met her green ones. Then the connection broke, and she smiled at Florence, her new BFF.

"We *must* hang out more often," I told Quinn.

"We must!" Quinn agreed, grinning.

The Divas and I smiled.

☆ ☆ ☆

"I'm home!" I yelled as I entered my house that afternoon.

"Hi, sweetie!" my parents yelled back, from the family room.

I went upstairs to my room. I wiggled the mouse of my computer to wake it up, then I immediately went online to check out what everyone was talking about. Everybody at my school has an online chat account, which makes it easier to keep up with the latest gossip. I follow everybody in my grade, but strictly for school purposes. It's not like I actually *care* what any of the unpopular kids are doing, I just want to know what they are saying about *me*.

Anyway, this was what I saw when I entered the chat:

Guys! Quinn is a Sassy Diva!!!!!

OMG. Why was Quinn hanging out with Vanessa, Adrienne, and Chelsea?

Does Vanessa like Quinn?!?!

JUST IN: Quinn = SASSY DIVA!!! And Vanessa REFUSES to let any NORMAL people join!

I wanted to clear up all the rumors right away. Quinn wasn't a Sassy Diva. She was still just a *Diva-in-Training*. Duh.

So this is what I posted:

Okay. So I can see that a lot of U R interested in the "Quinn-is-a-Sassy-Diva" rumors. I'm here to clear it all up. So, Quinn is NOT a Sassy Diva. That is all I will say.

I felt pretty satisfied. That was probably enough information to last at least one day of chatting among the gossip-hungry unpopular students, so I logged off and started on my homework.

Chapter Six

I shot out of bed like a rocket. I loved Fridays. After a breakfast of French toast, and my morning routine, I headed back upstairs to my room for the most important part of the morning—getting dressed. There were just so many cool outfits to choose from! But, since it was Friday, I decided to go a bit more casual. I decided on a pair of John Galliano shorts with a chic black tank top. For shoes, I wore some black Converse sneakers with cute hot pink laces. I was fashionably casual… or casually fashionable.

I arrived at school to find my Divas waiting for me by the circular drop-off driveway in front of the office. "Hey girls," I grinned.

"Hey Vanessa!" Adrienne and Chelsea chorused.

"Quinn's not here yet, by the way," Chelsea added. "You know, in case you were wondering where she was…"

"Okay…" I replied, obviously not interested.

We walked over to the wooden picnic tables and sat down. Before school started, we were always bored, though not as bored as we were in class. But finally, after a few long, boring minutes, Quinn showed up with a wide smile on her face. This time she was wearing an "I Love Ohio" shirt and baggy, rolled-up jeans. "Gross," Chelsea whispered. We watched Quinn as she put her stuff into her locker, then walked over to us.

"Hi girls," she smiled. She must have noticed that we were all staring at her outfit. She looked down at her shirt. "Do you like my top? I'm from Ohio, so I love wearing this. It's super comfy, too."

"Your top sucks," I answered, still staring at the "I Love Ohio" logo. *Don't. Think. Of Sixth. Grade.*

When I looked back up at her face, I noticed that Quinn's expression looked hurt. "That's why we're here to help you, stupid," I added, rolling my eyes.

Quinn grinned. She had probably chosen to ignore what I called her. I stood up.

"Take a look at *my* outfit," I said, striking a model pose. "Notice the super cute shorts. The rest of my outfit is casual. *This* is a 'super comfy' outfit, Quinn." I pointed to Adrienne. "Notice Adrienne's trendy-casual outfit. She is wearing a beige Gucci shirt and Dondup capris. If you haven't figured it out yet, today is Friday, so the Divas and I are going casual. See, Chelsea looks adorable in her 'I Love France' JC de Castelbajac shirt and her Rock and Republic black skinny jeans. *This* is what we call 'super comfy casual wear.'"

Quinn looked completely lost.

"Those are the names of designers," I snapped.

"Oh!" Quinn said happily. Then she frowned. "I don't own any designer clothes."

I almost had a heart attack. *No designer clothes!* I spun around to look at Adrienne and Chelsea. They were shocked too. "Not even a single pair of Uggs?" I asked Quinn.

"What are those?" Quinn replied.

"Omigosh," Adrienne murmured.

"I know, right?" Chelsea murmured back.

I shook my head, disappointed. "Well, Quinn. Since you're just a Diva-in-Training, you shouldn't undergo such a big change... *yet*. First we're going to focus on *acting* like a Sassy Diva. But we'll get to that during lunch, because we probably don't have enough time to—" The bell rang. "Start the lesson," I finished. I turned to my girls. "Well, guys, let's go to first period."

As I walked to class with my Sassy Divas, I could tell that today was going to be a long day. After all, the only thing about being a Sassy Diva that Quinn already knew how to do was to be confident, and smile.

☆ ☆ ☆

At lunch, we all met at our usual table. It was the most popular table. *Why?* Because it was right under a big, shady tree, and also because it was *our* table. I was excited to eat my amazing gourmet lobster sandwich. The Sassy Divas only ate gourmet food for lunch. It was basically an unspoken rule. Adrienne was eating a crunchy, spicy tuna hand roll, Chelsea was eating mini sliders, but Quinn was eating a ham sandwich! *How disgusting.* I studied the way Quinn ate. She took a huge bite, then rubbed some mustard off her lip with her finger. To make it even worse, she wiped her finger on her ratty old jeans.

"No! No! No!" I exclaimed, slamming my sandwich onto the table. The Sassy Divas stared. I used two fingers to point to Adrienne and Chelsea. "You two keep eating. I'm talking to Quinn." As soon as they started eating, I looked at Quinn, who was sitting across from me. "You're eating all wrong."

"I'm eating… all wrong?" Quinn looked confused.

"Yeah, that's exactly what I just said," I said, staring disgustedly at Quinn's mustard-covered hands. I looked into Quinn's eyes, and managed a smile. "But don't worry. Since the Sassy Divas are here, you are saved." I picked up my lobster sandwich. "First, you pick up your sandwich *carefully*. You don't want to get any sauce on your fingers. Then bring it to your mouth and take a small, ladylike bite." I took a tiny bite of my sandwich. "If you can eat a big bite without getting messy, then too bad, because you *must not* take a big bite. Take a small bite, like how I did." I took another careful bite, chewed, and swallowed. "Like that. If you get mustard on your hands, face, arms, or whatever, wipe it off with a napkin or go to the restroom and wash it off. Never, ever use your fingers! If you still smell like mustard, then spray on some perfume."

"Perfume…?" Quinn said, hesitantly.

"Yes, perfume! How many times do I need to repeat myself?" I snapped. "You must always carry pocket perfume! It's important to always smell good! How could you not know that, Quinn?"

Quinn stared at the ground as I took a deep breath. Chelsea and Adrienne shook their heads, obviously disappointed. *Who wouldn't be?*

"Quinn, in order to be a Sassy Diva, you *must* learn the rules," Chelsea emphasized. Quinn shrugged and went back to eating her sandwich. I was pleased to see that she was eating the way that I told her to.

A few minutes later, Adrienne decided to break the silence. "So Quinn!" she said. "What do you like to do in your spare time?"

"We all know the answer to that question," I said under my breath. Chelsea snickered.

"Well," Quinn began confidently. "I read a lot, and practice my math, and play with my frog and my cat."

I looked at Quinn in surprise. "You have a cat?"

Quinn nodded.

"So do I!" I grinned.

Quinn grinned back. "What breed?" she asked.

"A white Persian."

"Aww, cute! Mine is a white and brown Ragdoll."

"Adorable!"

Adrienne and Chelsea looked at me strangely. I didn't blame them.

"Now back to important stuff," I announced. "Your next lesson is 'How to Act Like a Sassy Diva.'"

We didn't finish all of the lessons during lunch that day, so we all went to Adrienne's house after school. Adrienne lives in a beautiful mansion with a big pool, and her parents are super sweet. As usual, her parents weren't home. Her father was a surgeon and her mother was an anesthesiologist, so they both worked super-long hours at the hospital. It was just the Sassy Divas... and Quinn. My plan for teaching Quinn how to act like a Sassy Diva was to just say or do things casually and see how she reacted. If she didn't react correctly, then I'd tell her what she did wrong.

"Your house is so pretty!" Quinn said, as she looked around.

Adrienne smiled. "Thanks."

"My house is better though," I stated.

Chelsea looked at me in shock. Adrienne looked offended. I quickly winked at them.

"Um, yeah!" Quinn said nervously. "Your house is probably... cooler... and stuff..."

Adrienne cleared her throat.

"I mean..." Quinn began, even more nervously. "Your house is really awesome too, Adrienne! Um..."

"Whose house is better?" I demanded.

"I, uh, I like b-both houses equally..."

"Make up your mind!" Adrienne exclaimed. Quinn looked so scared, I almost felt bad for her. But I sucked it up.

"Um..." Quinn's voice was shaky.

Adrienne started to giggle, which made me giggle, then Chelsea started giggling, and then the three of us were laughing. Quinn was so confused.

"What? I don't get it!" Quinn exclaimed.

"It was part of your test," Chelsea grinned.

Quinn laughed a relieved laugh.

"But," I said. "You have to learn what you did wrong."

"Okay." Quinn answered.

"You were way too insecure," I said. "You should always just give your honest opinion! If someone disagrees with you, don't change your mind or back down. Divas never worry about things like crushing other people's feelings. Honesty is the best choice."

"Okay," Quinn said.

"So now that Quinn has learned about honesty," Adrienne began, "who wants cake?" Everyone's hand shot up at once.

"Meeee!" Chelsea squealed.

We walked into Adrienne's large, sunlit kitchen and sat down at her rectangular glass dining table. Adrienne took four slices of strawberry shortcake out of the fridge and passed them around. Everyone ate properly. "Great job eating like a Sassy Diva, Quinn," Chelsea grinned.

Quinn blushed modestly. "Aww, thank you Chelsea." she quietly replied.

She wasn't "Miss Perfect" just yet. She definitely needed more attitude. I continued Quinn's lesson.

"Quinn, don't be so *soft*. My Sassy Divas are not marshmallows, sugar cookies, ice cream, whipped cream, or any other soft things. Understood?" Quinn nodded.

"Demand respect," Adrienne added.

"Adrienne's right," I pointed out. "You need to be respected."

Quinn nodded again.

"Yup," Chelsea agreed. "Quinn, what's your favorite color besides denim?"

"Umm… green?" Quinn answered.

"Like, regular green? Not lime green or forest green or something like that?" Chelsea asked.

"Yeah, I guess just regular green. And mustard yellow is pretty too."

"Ew!" Adrienne and I said together.

Quinn looked startled. Then her face turned red. "Well I *like* those colors. So, *whatever*!" she suddenly exclaimed.

I smiled. I had taught her well, but those colors still sucked. "I appreciate your Diva attitude," I said honestly. "But your favorite colors *need* to change." Quinn looked like she understood. "Adrienne?" I asked, "Paper, please. And a pen."

Adrienne came back a few seconds later with a clean sheet of binder paper and a fine-tip pink pen.

"I'm going to list some colors you can have as your favorites," I told Quinn.

Quinn's List of New Favorite Color Choices:

White

Sea green/mint green

Sky blue

Love. Vanessa

I handed Quinn the paper. "Gold is my favorite color, pink is Adrienne's, and dark purple is Chelsea's, so those colors are not included."

After reading the list, Quinn said, "I'll go with sky blue, that's a cute color."

"Agreed." Chelsea grinned.

"So Quinn, what do we do now that our cake is finished?" I asked.

Quinn lifted up her plate, ready to carry it to the sink. "We put our plates in the sink?"

The Sassy Divas and I laughed.

"That's Adrienne's job, silly!" I smiled. "We're the guests, remember?" Adrienne cleared our plates and wiped off the table.

"You need to remember that when you're the guest, you do not have to do any work," Chelsea said.

"She's right," I said. "Anyway," I smiled as I got up, "I must go. Quinn, I think you're all set for now. We'll get the supplies for your makeover later."

"M-makeover?" Quinn stammered.

"Huh?" Adrienne and Chelsea said at the same time.

"Yeah. Thank God we donate thirty bucks to the Sassy Diva bank account each month. We are gonna need to spend a lot of our savings to fix you up." I grinned. "See you girls tomorrow." I walked out of Adrienne's house, pleased with myself. Quinn was a proper Sassy Diva. All she needed now was to look like one.

Chapter Seven

Later that night, after finishing my homework, I went online.

I posted:

QUINN IS NOW A SASSY DIVA!

Then I checked my chat list and saw that Katie was online. I took this opportunity to annoy her.

VANESSA: Hey Katie.
KATIE: Ugh, Vanessa! What do you want?
VANESSA: I just wanted 2 let U know that Quinn is now a Sassy Diva.
KATIE: Oh great, so you poisoned her mind too?
VANESSA: We didn't poison her mind. She really likes us.
KATIE: Whatever. We never talked much anyway.

VANESSA: Maybe, but U wanted 2 B friends with her.

KATIE: Why do you say that?

VANESSA: It's obvious.

KATIE: It is not.

VANESSA: U 2 are both nerdy Bookworms, or at least U R.

KATIE: So you're saying that Quinn has changed?

VANESSA: Yup.

KATIE: Well okay, whatever.

VANESSA: Okay.

VANESSA: Bye.

I logged off. Katie was so annoying. I quickly sent a text to Adrienne and Chelsea, telling them to get online to video chat with me. I felt better the minute I entered the video chat with them. It was so good to see the faces of my *true* friends.

"Hey Vanessa," they said together. Adrienne was on her bed with her laptop, and Chelsea was at her desk, like me.

"So what's up?" Chelsea asked, twirling a strand of her dark auburn hair.

"Quinn's makeover," I announced.

"Okay, I had no idea we were gonna do this!" Chelsea protested.

"It's gonna be so hard!" Adrienne whined.

I sighed, irritated. "How could you two be so dumb?"

Adrienne pouted.

Chelsea looked offended.

"This is going to be so big, girls! It'll be our big break. Imagine what will happen when we make Quinn look amazing. Everyone will be all over us!" Adrienne's eyes lit up. "So here's what we're gonna do. We're not going to use designer clothes because that is not really Quinn's thing," I began. "Adrienne, you are in charge of her accessories. Chelsea, you do her makeup. I'll be in charge of her outfit styling."

"What's Quinn's style gonna be, though?" Chelsea snickered. "Geek?"

"Shut up, Chelsea!" Adrienne argued. "V knows what she's doing."

I rolled my eyes at Chelsea. "Geek-*chic*, actually."

Chelsea smiled. "Awesome."

"Gather your supplies over the week. We'll meet next Friday after school, my house. Remember, *geek-chic*."

"So, like, flannel shirts," Adrienne suggested.

"And nerdy glasses," Chelsea told Adrienne.

"I figured that one out on my *own*, thank you very much!" Adrienne snapped.

"Jeez, I was just trying to be helpful." Chelsea replied.

I rested my head on my propped-up hand, "Have you guys ever noticed that Quinn's eyes are like emeralds?"

Chelsea smiled. "I know, right?"

"They're beautiful," Adrienne agreed. "They add that perfect touch of color to her face. Kinda like Chelsea's auburn hair."

"Heh. Thanks," Chelsea blushed.

"Anyway, is everyone good?" I asked.

"Yeah," Adrienne and Chelsea replied.

"Awesome. See you guys later." I logged off. *This was going to be great.*

Chapter Eight

On Monday, everybody was talking about Quinn being the newest Sassy Diva. I listened to the excited voices chattering as I strolled down the long hallway to my locker.

"Did you hear about Quinn?"

"She's a Sassy Diva, can you believe it?"

"Wait...isn't she that nerdy new girl?"

"She was, but now she's totally cool!"

"Oh my god!"

"I know. The Sassy Divas are so fabulous!"

Someone tapped my shoulder. I turned around. A skinny, freckle-faced girl was looking at me. "May I help you?" I asked.

"I hear Quinn's in the Sassy Divas now," she said quietly.

I stared at her for a few seconds before replying. "Yeah she is. So?"

"Er..." the girl hesitated awkwardly. I was getting really impatient.

"Quinn's in the Sassy Divas! Did you want to join or something?"

"Can I..." she began.

"NO, YOU CANNOT!" I yelled. "GO AWAY!" She hurried away, sobbing.

Jeez, some people were so nosy! I continued walking. Adrienne and Chelsea ran up next to me.

"Oh... My... Gosh..." Chelsea began.

"So many people have been bothering us today about Quinn," Adrienne finished.

"So annoying," Chelsea added.

"Understood," I said, nodding my head. "Speaking of, where is Quinn anyways?"

"I dunno," Adrienne answered. "Does she have a cell?"

"Duh!" I said. I took out my cell phone and punched in her number.

Quinn answered her phone on the first ring, "Hey, Vanessa!"

"Quinn," I snapped. "Where the heck are you?'

"The library. Don't worry though, I'm not actually reading. I'm just looking at the pictures in cookbooks."

"I don't care! Sassy Divas look for recipes *online*. Get your butt over to the hallway A.S.A.P. We are standing in front of room eight."

"Okay! Okay!" She hung up.

After a few minutes, Quinn joined us.

"You're a Sassy Diva, Quinn! A SASSY DIVA!" I scolded.

"I know! I'm honored…" Quinn blushed.

"Well we're a *clique*. We stay together when we're at school." Quinn looked embarrassed.

"Sorry…" she offered.

I rolled my eyes.

"And Quinn, tonight you will not be with us, 'cause we'll be shopping for you."

Quinn nodded.

"Tomorrow is geek-chic makeover day. I expect to see you all at my house at 1:30 pm sharp. We have a lot of work to do, so *don't* be late!" I declared. I turned around and clapped my hands together. "We're all set?" The girls nodded. "Awesome. Let's enjoy our day!"

That evening, Ryan was the one who called me.

"Hey, Ryan!" I greeted him happily.

"Uh, Vanessa?"

"Say hi."

"Hi. Vanessa?"

"What's up?"

"Everyone at school was talking about Quinn being a new member of the Sassy Divas."

"Yeah, she is! Isn't it exciting?"

"Why did you make her a member? She's still wearing those big glasses. I thought you wouldn't like that."

"I don't. We're actually giving her a makeover this weekend, Ryan."

"Oh. Do you even *like* her?"

I let out a light laugh. "Not really."

"Aren't the Sassy Divas your set group of friends? I thought you don't let new girls join."

"Well, yeah, we normally don't. But we're just using Quinn. We're using her to make Katie crawl back to us."

"That's not very nice."

"No one *said* it was!" I retorted, rolling my eyes.

Ryan sighed. "Good luck, I guess…"

"Thanks," I smiled. "I wish I could give you a big hug through the phone."

Ryan laughed. "And I wish I could hug you back through the phone."

I laughed too. "Bye, Ryan."

"Bye, V."

✩ ✩ ✩

That Friday night, Adrienne, Chelsea, and I went shopping for Quinn. We found everything we needed. I was confident that the makeover would go the way we planned. I was in such a good mood that after shopping, I decided to be nice to my mom and watch a little bit of TV with her (just not that boring show about the weird addictions).

"Honey?" my mom asked, during the commercial break.

"Yeah?" I replied, reaching for a fresh handful of popcorn.

"How's everything going with your friends?"

"Good. We have a new addition to the Sassy Divas." I passed the popcorn bowl to my mom.

"Who is she?" she asked.

"The new girl at school. Her name is Quinn."

"Well, congratulations! That's a pretty name. I look forward to meeting her."

"Thanks," I replied.

✩ ✩ ✩

"Welcome!" I grinned as I opened the door for Adrienne. The light from the afternoon sun spilled onto our white marble floor. She smiled as she walked in, carrying a huge bag filled with accessories.

"We'll be right here in the living room today," I said. Adrienne took a seat on the plush velvet couch. "Did you bring the nerd glasses?" I asked.

"Yup! Shiny black ones," Adrienne said proudly. "They go with, like, any outfit."

After a few minutes, there was a knock at the door. I looked through the peephole. It was Chelsea, holding a large makeup case. I opened the door, glancing at my cell phone. It was already 1:32 pm. "You're late," I snapped.

Chelsea shuffled in, sheepishly mumbling, "Sorry."

"And of course, Quinn's late too!" I exclaimed, throwing my hands in the air. I glared at Chelsea. "I expect better from you." Chelsea looked ashamed. "Whatever." I sighed. "Quinn's not even here yet anyways." We sat down on the couch next to Adrienne.

A few minutes later, we heard a lot of loud knocking at my door and a voice yelling, "Oh my gosh! I'm sorry! I'm sorry I'm late! Let me in! Please!" I rolled my eyes, sighed, and went to open the door. Quinn rushed in. I put a hand on her shoulder, leading her towards the living room.

"Quinn," I began. "I'm gonna go easy on you because you're a new Sassy Diva. But you need to be on time! Always! Understand?"

"Understood," Quinn said with a nod.

I clapped my hands together. "Let's get this makeover started!"

The Sassy Divas cheered.

"I thought we should start with the fashion first, like they do on my favorite show, *What Not to Wear*," I said. Adrienne and Chelsea nodded in agreement.

"Awesome," Quinn grinned.

I gestured to three large Nordstrom shopping bags that sat on the wooden coffee table. "Your brand new wardrobe is right here." I pointed to the first bag. "This bag is filled with tops!" I announced. I pulled out a baby blue plaid flannel shirt. "Lots of flannel shirts!" I threw the shirt at Quinn. I pulled out a white tank top with spaghetti straps. "Plus lots of tank tops to wear under your new flannel shirts!" I threw the tank top at Quinn too. "And there are some other shirts in there too." Then I pointed to the second bag. "That bag is filled with pants. Jeans, shorts, skirts... you know." I pulled out a pair of black skinny jeans. And yes, I threw the jeans at Quinn. "And of course, we saved the best for last!" I exclaimed, pointing to the third bag. "Shoes! We have Converse for you, in a ton of different colors. And you get a special pair of sparkly black TOMS." I pulled out black glitter TOMS, but decided not to throw those at Quinn. Instead I walked up to her and placed them next to the pile of clothes I had thrown at her.

"Thanks for not throwing *those* at me," Quinn snapped. Then she winked at me. "But seriously, thanks Vanessa. You're awesome." I smiled. She was right, I was awesome.

"By the way Quinn, you *do* know geek-chic style, right?" I asked.

"Oh yeah," Quinn said. "I did research after you told me today was 'geek-chic makeover day!'"

"You like it and everything?"

"Yup."

"Awesome," I grinned. I looked at Adrienne, "Your turn."

Adrienne picked up her accessory bag and happily walked over to stand next to me in the center of the living room. She set the bag down beside her, and pulled out a pair of square, black, nerd glasses. "These," she said excitedly, "are your nerd glasses. Without these, you would not have a complete geek-chic look." Adrienne put them back in her bag and pulled out a cute contact lens case. "This is where your contact lenses live." Quinn squealed with delight.

"Yaaayy! Contact lenses! You guys totally ROCK!" Adrienne, Chelsea, and I smiled at each other. We knew we rocked. And everyone knew I rocked the most.

"Those contact lenses were my idea," I proudly informed Quinn. "I even had my mom call your mom to find out what your exact prescription was." Quinn beamed gratefully at me.

"When you wear these," Adrienne said, holding up a pair of contacts. "You just put your nerd glasses on over them, since the nerd glasses have no prescription. They're just for looks, obviously."

"Do you actually know how to wear contacts?" Chelsea asked.

Quinn nodded. "I've practiced at the eye doctor's. They told me I needed to practice if I ever wanted to get them."

"Anyway," Adrienne continued loudly, putting the contact lenses back into the bag. "This bag is filled with fun accessories like jewelry, belts, hats, and *this*." Adrienne pulled out a bright orange purse. "This is your purse." Quinn squealed again. Adrienne handed the purse and accessory bag to Quinn. Then she sat back down on the couch.

Chelsea walked to the center of the room and opened up her enormous purple makeup case. "Okay," Chelsea said. "In this case, I have a bunch of awesome stuff. There is an eyeshadow palette with practically every color of eyeshadow that is flattering for green eyes. There's also mascara, light-colored lipgloss and lipstick, light pink blush, concealer... and much more. Light colors are way easier to put on, and more flattering. You can ask me for help, or use YouTube for makeup tutorials. Oh, and stay away from the fake lashes. You will not be able to pull them off. That's about everything you need to know, got it?" Chelsea finished. Quinn nodded.

"Okay!" I said, "Time for the fashion show! Quinn, go change. Wear the stuff I threw at you, your nerd glasses, and put on your contacts." Quinn grabbed the pile of clothes, the contacts, and her nerd glasses, and went into the bathroom to change.

"This is so exciting," Chelsea said happily.

"I know!" Adrienne agreed. "We should make her walk down the hallway slowly and then pose when she reaches the living room!"

"That would be cool," Chelsea grinned.

"Girls!" I exclaimed. "We don't do cheesy. She'll just walk to us normally!" The girls looked down.

After a couple minutes of awkward silence, Quinn walked down the hall and into the living room. She looked great! Adrienne, Chelsea, and I gave her a standing ovation. She blushed and smiled. "The first geek-chic member of the Sassy Divas!" I grinned.

Quinn bowed. "Thanks so much, guys. I feel so pretty!" she said happily.

"You look pretty, too," Chelsea pointed out.

"Well girls," I smiled. "Great work! We've transformed Quinn! Now get out of my house. I want to enjoy my Saturday."

Disappointed, the other Sassy Divas gathered up their things and slowly left the house. I slammed the door behind them and smiled. I felt like a magical fairy.

Chapter Nine

Monday, at school, Quinn was wearing the same outfit she had changed into on Saturday. We were the new and improved Sassy Divas, with a brand-new addition who happened to be both pretty and stylish, thanks to me, Vanessa Pocker! And of course, she got a lot of compliments.

"Whoa, Quinn! You look cute!" other students would say.

"Oh, thank you!" I would grin back. "I gave her a big makeover."

They would look at me funny and leave. But then Katie came up to us.

"Hi Quinn!" she smiled, ignoring me.

"Um, hello?" I said. Katie kept ignoring me.

"Hey Katie. What's up?" Quinn asked.

"Can you please give me some fashion tips?" Katie asked Quinn. I was horrified.

"Um, I am right here! I gave Quinn a makeover! Everything was done by me!"

Katie looked straight into my eyes. "I. Don't. Care." *Oh my gosh, she's giving me Sassy Diva attitude! I knew she was always meant to be a Sassy Diva, not a Bookworm!*

"You wannabe Sassy Diva!" I spat.

Katie looked puzzled. "Um, excuse me?" I felt like I was going to cry. Katie missed me. I *knew* she did.

"You miss me." I smiled sadly. "You want to be a Sassy Diva again!"

"Um..." she hesitated.

"It's okay, Katie! I'll think about it! Do you want to eat lu—"

"Vanessa?"

"...Five members would be okay, I think..."

"Vanessa!"

I looked at Katie. "Yeah?"

"I *don't* miss you. I'm actually better off without some brat like you telling me what to do, what to wear, and how to act."

"That's not what Vanessa does!" Adrienne yelled.

"She *helps* us!" Chelsea yelled.

Katie rolled her eyes. "Sorry, V. I mean, Vanessa." Then she left.

I bolted into the girls' restroom and locked myself in a stall so nobody would see me crying. *Stupid Katie.*

Later that night, I went online to check everyone's posts.

One post read:

Omg. Quinn looked amazing today!

So I commented:

I know. I gave her a makeover.

Another post read:

Quinn is a fashionista. She would be better off without Vanessa.

I screamed, "No, no, no, no, *no!*" Immediately, my mom and dad burst through my bedroom door. "Sweetie, what's wrong?" my mom asked.

"Oh, um... it's nothing... I, uh, I just learned that... er... Michael Jackson died...?" I replied.

"But Michael Jackson died back in 2009, Vanessa," my dad said, looking confused and a little concerned.

"Well, I just found out about it." I responded, defensively.

"Vanessa, it was all over the news, and plastered on every magazine cover!" my dad continued.

"Whatever!" I cut him off. "I'm fine now. You guys can just go. Please."

My parents exchanged a worried look, but left. I was mad at CuddleBunny64 (whoever that was) for posting such a horrible thing.

So, I posted:

OMG THAT IS SO STUPID! QUINN'S A FASHIONISTA THANKS TO ME! I WENT SHOPPING FOR HER OKAY?! SHE WOULD NOT BE BETTER OFF WITHOUT ME. I MADE ALL OF THIS HAPPEN! I DON'T WANT TO HEAR THAT EVER AGAIN!

Perfect. That would shut them up. I read a few more old posts. At least Quinn had been responding to the compliments by telling people that her new style was all my idea. I couldn't believe that other people actually thought Quinn was as talented as me when it came to fashion. I checked my chat list and found that Ryan was online. I immediately started chatting with him.

VANESSA: Ryan!

RYAN: What now?

VANESSA: Everyone is saying that Quinn looked great in her outfit today, but they're giving Quinn the credit and not me! I was the one who gave the girl the makeover!!

RYAN: ...

VANESSA: And someone said that Quinn would be better off WITHOUT me!

RYAN: Ouch.

VANESSA: I KNOW. Without me, Quinn would be nothing! NOTHING!

RYAN: Yeah.

VANESSA: She'd still be walking around in those old-lady glasses and gross outfits! But since she has me, the Queen of the School, she is wearing trendy clothes and has her emerald eyes on display! She looks BEAUTIFUL now, ALL THANKS TO ME, and I'm not getting an OUNCE of credit!!!

RYAN: I'm so sorry to hear that, V. I know how it feels to not get credit for something that's very important to you. Once, I wrote this really nice poem, and some kid named Mike at school said that it was his poem, but it wasn't! It eventually got cleared up though, and everyone knew that I wrote it.

VANESSA: Ryan, my problem is actually important.

RYAN: Mine was super important too! You know what Mike could've done? He could've sent it off to get it published somewhere! And let's say some big publisher really liked it and wanted to put it in an collection of the best poems from young authors in Los Angeles—then Mike would have gotten the credit that I deserved for something I wrote myself!

VANESSA: It's just a poem, Ryan. Chill. Besides, now people know that it was YOUR poem, and not his.

RYAN: But don't people know that it was actually you who did all that?

VANESSA: I'm trying to make it known among the normal kids. U can count on them to tell it to the social outcasts and such.

RYAN: So everyone will know in no time. Relax, V. There are starving children in this world, and you're worried about getting credit for some makeover you gave to a new student.

VANESSA: Ugh, fine, I'll shut up.

RYAN: Alright, so how was the rest of your day?

VANESSA: OH! I almost forgot! Guess what else happened?

RYAN: There's a huge "Buy 1 Get 1 Half Off" sale at that designer shoe store you like?

VANESSA: DSW? I wish!

RYAN: Then what is it?

VANESSA: So, Katie was acting like a total Diva today, right?

RYAN: Uh-huh.

VANESSA: And so I'm like, "OMG! Katie totally misses me! She wants to be a Sassy Diva again!" I have NO IDEA what went over me, but I started acting super desperate! I was like, "There's room for U! U can hang with us during lunch! I knew U missed me!" and then she's all, "Actually, Vanessa, I don't miss U! I don't need some brat telling me what to do!" She totally dissed me!! I hate her, Ryan, I HATE HER! And to make it worse, I had to stay in the bathroom for a while because I was CRYING.

RYAN: Vanessa, maybe you should just tell Katie that you really do miss her. Who knows, maybe she secretly misses you on the inside too!

VANESSA: Ryan, she dissed me. Friends don't diss friends.

RYAN: Isn't that what you've been doing this whole entire time?

VANESSA: That's different! I just want her to see how much she needs me! I'm trying to mold our friendship back into place!

RYAN: By using her friend against her?

VANESSA: U wouldn't understand. I know what I'm doing, Ryan.

RYAN: If you say so! Sorry, though, I gotta go now. Catch you later, V!

☆ ☆ ☆

The next day, during science class, I saw Katie writing something on a piece of light yellow paper.

It didn't look science-related. Then she passed it to Quinn. After class, I made Quinn show me the note. It said:

Dear Quinn,

I love your clothes. Super-cute! So I know you're a Sassy Diva and all, but do you want to get smoothies after school? And maybe we can do homework together, if you want.

Sincerely, Katie

"Oh my gosh!" I was shaking. I felt like screaming. I glared at Quinn. "No! You are not going talk to her!" I commanded. "Argh!"

Chelsea and Adrienne looked at me, then glanced at each other nervously.

"I need to be alone!" I yelled. "Go away." The Sassy Divas walked away quickly.

Chapter Ten

At home that night, my cell phone rang while I was in the middle of drawing an old-fashioned boutique. I had created an adorable sketch of the storefront, and I was drawing some detailed pictures of the inside. I looked at the caller ID. It was Quinn. "Hey Quinn," I answered, putting down my pencil.

"Hey V," she said happily.

"What's up?"

"I just wanted to give you an idea that I had. For, like, a Sassy Diva party."

"Ooh, a Sassy Diva party. I like that. What's your idea?"

"Well, we meet up at your house and go to the mall. We spend the day at the mall. Then, for dinner, we can eat at…"

"My house!" I offered. "We can eat at my house. My mom is a great cook!"

"Okay, that works!"

"Maybe we can even have a sleepover! A Sassy Diva sleepover!"

"Oh my gosh, perfect!"

I grinned. "So we'll meet up at my house and then head to the mall. We spend the day at the mall and eat dinner at my house. Then we'll have a sleepover! Ohmygosh, I'm so smart!"

"You are, Vanessa!" Quinn agreed.

"Quinn, I have to tell Adrienne and Chelsea. Get online as soon as you can. I'll chat when I'm ready."

"Okay. Bye, V!"

"Bye Quinn."

I hung up and went back to working on my drawing. It took me about twenty minutes to finish it. I loved to draw, to be honest. I dreamed of becoming a fashion designer someday, so my drawings usually had something to do with fashion, shopping, or style. After I finished my drawing, I went online to chat. Adrienne and Chelsea were already online. They were always online. I chatted with them.

VANESSA: Adrienne? Chelsea? I need 2 tell U guys something important.

CHELSEA: Ooh, important!

ADRIENNE: What's up?

VANESSA: Sassy Diva sleepover. That's what.

CHELSEA: OMG!

ADRIENNE: OMG, I love sleepovers!

VANESSA: We just have 2 figure out a date.

ADRIENNE: What day is it 2day?

VANESSA: Tuesday.

CHELSEA: I have no plans on Friday night or Saturday morning.

ADRIENNE: Neither do I.

VANESSA: One sec, let me invite Quinn to the chat.

-Quinn has entered-

QUINN: Hey girls!

ADRIENNE: Hey Quinn!

CHELSEA: Hi Quinn!

VANESSA: Quinn, R U free Friday night and Saturday morning?

QUINN: Let me check my calendar....

CHELSEA: V, R U planning on having your mom pick us up from school?

VANESSA: No. I want to freshen up at home. And U guys should too.

ADRIENNE: Yeah. Nothing beats a warm lavender-scented bubble bath.

QUINN: I'm free!

CHELSEA: Yay!

VANESSA: Awesome!

ADRIENNE: Guys, I gotta go. I'll C U guys 2morrow!!!

QUINN: Bye!

CHELSEA: C ya!

VANESSA: I actually have 2 go 2. Bye!

I signed out and went downstairs to find my mom and dad watching *My Strange Addiction*, my mom's stupid favorite show. "Hey Mom? Dad? This Friday night, can Adrienne, Chelsea, and Quinn come over for a Sassy Divas sleepover?"

"Of course, darling," Mom said. "Come watch this show with us—"

"Okay, thanks a lot Mom!" I interrupted loudly, ignoring the last thing she said. I ran up the stairs to my room and started a new sketch.

✩ ✩ ✩

The rest of the week flew by, and before I knew it, it was Friday afternoon. I smiled widely as I admired my reflection in my full-length mirror. I had just finished getting ready. My hair was gathered into a high ponytail. I was wearing a dainty dress with a bird pattern on it by Free People and a pair of golden Jimmy Choo sandals. I looked amazing.

The doorbell rang. I hurried downstairs and opened the door. "Hey Quinn!" She walked inside with her bag. "We can put your bag upstairs," I smiled, picking up her duffel bag. We went up to my room.

"This is gonna be so much fun!" Quinn declared.

I smiled. "Definitely. What stores at the mall do you want to check out first?"

"I hope you don't mind if we check out some, like, non-designer clothing stores…"

"Oh no, don't worry about it. We'll be happy to help you shop. Besides, I don't get most of my clothes at the mall."

"You don't?" Quinn looked surprised.

"Not at *this* mall. I mean, I get, like, *basics* from this mall…"

"Oh okay, I see. Thanks, V!"

I smiled. "No problem. Hey, Quinn, let's go downstairs so we can answer the door quicker when the other Divas get here."

Quinn and I went downstairs and sat on the couch. I could smell Alfredo sauce coming from the kitchen, where my mom was cooking. *Mmm. Dinner.*

"So what stores *do* you go to at the mall?" Quinn asked.

"I love Icing. They have a bunch of really cute accessories," I said.

"Ohmygosh, I totally love Icing too!" Quinn grinned.

"Really?"

"Yeah! I like Abercrombie too. I bought some flannel shirts there." Quinn said.

"Yeah, their stuff is cute. I, of course, love Sephora too."

"Ah, yes. Their blue lipgloss is pretty epic," agreed Quinn.

"Yeah! It's even better if you put it on over red lipstick. It makes your teeth look whiter."

"Wow."

"I know. Oh, and I love Forever 21."

"Oh, yeah, that store's pretty awesome. What do you think of Aeropostale?"

"Uh… it's okay." I replied. Aeropostale was kind of cheap-looking for my taste. But other than that, I was really surprised that we liked so many of the same stores at the mall. "Quinn, we have pretty similar taste! How cool!"

Then the doorbell rang. I got up to answer it. It was Adrienne and Chelsea. I greeted them and took their bags upstairs, while they waited with Quinn.

"Mrs. Pocker, the food smells terrific!" I heard Adrienne say as I came back down the stairs.

"What are you making?"Chelsea asked. I took my place on the couch next to my Sassy Divas.

"Fettuccine Alfredo with veggies and shrimp!" my mom beamed.

"Ooh, yum," Chelsea smiled.

"And it's ready!" my mom said proudly. "Take a seat, girls, we're having an early dinner tonight."

✩ ✩ ✩

"V, are diamond studs still in style?" Chelsea asked me, as she browsed through the earrings rack at Icing.

"No," I said as I looked at the headbands. "That's so *Christmas*, Chelsea!"

My mom had just dropped us off at the mall. Our first stop was Icing. Since hoops were totally out, I was looking around to see what should be the next trend.

"The chunky rings are really cute," Adrienne said.

"Ooh, they are," Quinn said softly.

"Ah-ha!" I grinned. I picked up a skinny black headband with a floppy black bow. "Girls, we need to get bow headbands trending! They're super cute!"

The Sassy Divas looked my way and smiled. "Love it!" Chelsea said happily.

"Very cute," Adrienne agreed.

"I want one…" Quinn smiled.

"Don't worry guys, I'll buy one for each of you, as long as we get them trending."

"Aww, thanks, V!" Adrienne said.

I smiled and took the headbands to the cash register. The cashier was a skinny girl who looked like she was probably in her early twenties. "So you're the trendsetter at your school?" she asked, smiling.

"Yes," I said proudly.

"Mmhmm. Interesting." She gave me a small bag filled with our headbands. "There you go. Enjoy the rest of your day."

I took the bag. "Ready, girls?"

"Yeah," the Sassy Divas responded.

"Let's go to the next store!" I declared, smiling.

"I seriously loved the peacock feather headbands," Quinn said, as we walked.

"I know!" I beamed. "We should make them the next trend."

"Definitely. And those headbands with the little hats? Adorable!" exclaimed Chelsea.

"We need to get those for the next school dance," I decided. "They look really cute if you know what to wear them with!"

"Totally!" Quinn agreed. The two of us laughed. Adrienne and Chelsea looked at us weirdly.

"Oh, Quinn, we need to do this more often," I smiled at her, and she smiled back. Then I noticed that the other two girls were awkwardly silent. So I changed the subject. "Okay. Next up: Sephora!" I announced.

"I say we get a bunch of makeup and give each other awesome makeovers at home! And we can, like, dress up and stuff!" Quinn grinned, clapping her hands excitedly. I gave her a high five. *Another weird look from Adrienne and Chelsea.*

"Great idea, Quinn. Let's do it," I said, ignoring the weird behavior from Adrienne and Chelsea.

Sephora was pretty crowded, as usual. The first thing we did was test out the rack of lipgloss samples. We tried on the pinks, reds, and even the purples.

"Pucker up!" Adrienne told Chelsea. She put some red lipstick on her. "Beautiful!"

Chelsea looked in the mirror and smiled.

"Ooh, ooh!" Quinn grinned. She looked at me. "Okay, now *you* pucker up!" She put lipgloss on my lips. "There!" Quinn grinned. She covered her mouth to keep herself from laughing. I looked in the mirror quickly to find dark purple lipgloss smeared across my lips. I laughed, then grabbed a tissue to wipe it off.

Next, we went to the eye makeup section.

"I want to get every color of glitter eyeliner!" Chelsea said as she stared at the glittery eyeliner. It was perfect for Chelsea. She loved glitter and unusual eye makeup. "As soon as I test it out," she added, picking out a glittery midnight blue eyeliner stick and walking over to the mirror.

After trying it out, Chelsea walked back over to me. "Yeah, I'm definitely getting this!"

"No," I told her. "Midnight blue is *so* out. Get some other color, like royal purple!"

"But I *like* this one..."

"Chelsea." I raised my eyebrows. Chelsea disappointedly put the eyeliner down.

Lastly, we went to the perfume section. We tested so many of them that we reeked of perfume by the time we walked out with our bags of new makeup.

"That was so much fun!" Quinn grinned. She inhaled. "Mmm, Vanessa, you smell like chocolate!"

"It's *Angel* perfume," Adrienne smiled and winked. "V's wearing it 'cause she's such a total 'angel'."

We all laughed.

✮ ✮ ✮

"What movie should we watch?" I asked, scrolling through the On Demand list. We were sprawled on our sleeping bags in front of the TV, wearing our pajamas.

"*Twilight!*" Chelsea suggested.

"Yeah!" Adrienne agreed. Then she turned to look at Quinn. "What do you wanna watch?"

Quinn shrugged. "I'll watch whatever you guys want to watch. I love pretty much all movies!"

Adrienne turned back to me. "Yeah, so let's watch *Twilight* then."

"No," I frowned. "I've already seen *Twilight* way too many times. How about... *The Clique!* I love that movie. It inspires me."

"*Harry Potter?*" Quinn suggested.

"No way!" I said. "We're watching *The Clique.*" I pressed play and turned to my Sassy Divas. "Ice cream, anyone?"

The next morning, we woke up bright and early. "Girls!" My mom called from the kitchen. "Breakfast's almost ready!" We hurried into the dining room and took our seats at the table. From my favorite chair, I could see my mom hurrying around the kitchen in her yellow-checkered apron, checking the pans on the stove, pulling syrups out of the fridge, and grabbing plates out of the cupboards.

"I love pancakes!" Adrienne smiled.

"I feel kinda bad that your mom is preparing each of our pancakes just the way we want them!" Quinn said to me. "At my house, everyone has to eat the same thing. No special orders."

"Oh, don't worry, honey," My mom said sweetly, brushing her dark blonde hair out of her face as she poked her head out from the kitchen. "I'm used to it. Vanessa is very particular. Besides, we already have everything she likes—blueberry pancakes, whipped cream, strawberries, bananas, vanilla yogurt with granola—and we already have chocolate chips, which I melted for Chelsea, butter, maple syrup, and regular pancakes!"

"Oh," Quinn smiled. "Thanks."

"No problem!" My mom said, ducking back into the kitchen. She came back into the dining room, balancing a tray piled with our plates. Three pancakes with whipped cream, chocolate chips, and sliced strawberries for Quinn. Two pancakes buttered with maple syrup and covered in whipped cream for Adrienne. Pancakes dripping with melted chocolate and whipped cream, strawberries, bananas, and blueberries for Chelsea. I was having my signature dish, which was blueberry pancakes with whipped cream, strawberries, bananas, and of course, vanilla yogurt with granola. After serving us, my mom wiped off her brow with a smile. "If you girls need anything else, let me know. I'll be reading in my room." We hungrily devoured our pancakes.

"Girls," I announced, as I put our plates in the sink, "Monday at school, we all need to wear our bow headbands. We'll start trending them right away."

"Okay," Adrienne smiled.

We washed up and got dressed, then spent the rest of the day rating outfits in my magazines and talking about new trends. It had been another great Sassy Diva day.

Chapter Eleven

At school, we were told we were going to have a final test on the book *Treasure Island*. Of course, final tests are important, which explains why Quinn desperately sent me a bunch of video chat requests. After making her wait for about an hour while I painted my toenails, I finally accepted one.

"Yes, Quinn?" I smiled as I screwed the nail polish cap back on. The color was a pale shade of coral, which was totally trending right now.

"Oh my gosh Vanessa! I totally need your help! Where do I start studying? Should I start with vocab or the actual info? How should I quiz myself?" she blurted out super- fast. "Ohmygosh, the test is in *two days—*"

"Calm down, Quinn. It's just another test," I interrupted, rolling my eyes, then glancing down. My toes looked fabulous.

Quinn gasped. "Vanessa... it's a final!"

"Well, just do what I do!"

Quinn looked at me eagerly.

"Cheat!" I finished happily.

Quinn gaped. "What?!"

"Cheat! C-H-E-A-T. Cheat."

"I can't cheat!"

I sighed. "Why not?"

"*Cheating—*"

"Writing on your arm," I corrected.

"Writing on your arm," Quinn snapped back. "Can lead to getting caught."

"Ooh, scary."

"Getting caught means being sent to the principal's office."

"Yeah, so?"

"Going to the principal's office equals TROUBLE."

I sighed. "Listen, Quinn. Going to the principal's office means that Mr. Mandell will lecture you and then give you a punishment. Plus, the punishments are dumb, like 'you can't go to extended care next Tuesday', or, 'you can't participate in Pajama Day' or whatever. *Not* a big deal."

"But... I just... I just can't, V. I can't," Quinn said.

I shrugged. "If you don't write on your arm you'll get a bad grade. But whatevs."

"A bad grade? Pfft. Please."

"An F, Quinn. If you don't write on your arm, you'll get a big fat F on your paper. And I'll rub my perfect score in your face. You might feel bad, or cry, but guess what, Quinn? I'll make sure that *no one* comforts you. 'Cause you didn't listen to me."

Quinn looked afraid. I shrugged and picked up a purple gel pen. "Write, Quinn. You know you want to... think of the A-plus. The perfect score." I dangled the gel pen in front of my webcam. Quinn looked down.

"Well, I better start *studying*," I winked. "See you tomorrow." I ended the video chat.

☆ ☆ ☆

On the day of the test, I found Quinn with Adrienne and Chelsea.

Adrienne looked over my outfit and gasped. "*Love* the shoes, V."

I smiled and looked at my shoes. "Thanks. They're Zigi Soho Cupcake Flats."

"Super cute," Chelsea agreed.

"Anyway," I went on. "So did you guys all write on your arms?"

They all nodded. Quinn smiled and rolled up the sleeve of her flannel shirt to prove it.

"Impressive," I smiled back at Quinn.

"Don't you think it'll be kind of hard for Quinn to cheat since she sits up near the front of the class?" Adrienne suggested.

Quinn froze. "Oh *crud*!"

"No worries!" I grinned extra wide with artificial cheeriness. I gave Quinn a look that told her to shut up.

The bell rang.

✩ ✩ ✩

During Literature, Quinn was as nervous as a moth being held by the wing. She gave me a desperate look. I gave her a look that said *Oh, come on.*

Our Literature teacher, Miss Roze, walked to her desk and slipped on her glasses. Miss Roze was my favorite teacher at school. She totally pulled off the whole chic-office look. Her dark hair was pulled into a messy bun. She was wearing a ruffled lilac blouse and a grey pencil skirt that fit her like a glove, with dainty nude heels. "Okay, students," she smiled, looking up at all of us. "We are going to start the test in a moment." She picked up a stack of papers and passed them out. "This is the *Treasure Island* final... no cheating, write the name, date, period... you all know the drill." Miss Roze walked back to her desk. "Pencils ready? Begin."

Sitting behind Quinn gave me an advantage. I glanced up at her to see if she was looking at her arm. She wasn't. *She's probably waiting for the right moment,* I thought. I slowly rolled up my sleeve and filled out some of the answers on the test. I glanced at Quinn again. Her eyes darted toward the inside of her arm. I saw her scribble some words on the paper. *Good,* I thought. I went back to my test.

It was awfully quiet, so I was startled when Miss Roze yelled, "Quinn!" I lifted up my head in a flash and stared at Quinn. She was shaking.

"You think you can just cheat and not get caught?" Miss Roze said angrily. "Do I look that stupid to you? Goodness, looking at answers written on your arm! Go to the principal's office!" Quinn was in shock. She didn't move an inch. I could imagine the thoughts going through her head. "What are you waiting for? Move!" Quinn slowly got up and trudged out of the room, shooting me a dirty look on her way out.

"The rest of you, finish your test," Miss Roze said. I kept my head down and didn't look at my arm for the rest of the test.

At lunch, Quinn wasn't happy. It was the first time we had seen each other after Literature. Adrienne and Chelsea bounced along with us, gossiping about some new reality show. I wasn't paying attention.

We all sat down at our usual spot.

"You guys haven't said a word," Chelsea mumbled, redoing her ponytail. She was referring to me and Quinn, obviously.

"*I* have a good reason," Quinn snapped.

"Spill," Adrienne said.

I took a long gulp of my peach-flavored iced tea.

Quinn sighed. "To make the long story short, I got in big trouble, thanks to Vanessa."

"Sheesh, you guys are acting like third-graders," Chelsea replied, unscrewing her water bottle.

"Shut up," I snarled angrily. "Besides, it's *Quinn* who's acting like the third-grader!"

"Not true!" Quinn protested.

"Okay, okay, okay!" Adrienne said loudly. "Tell me the whole story."

Quinn explained everything, starting from our chat session. She seemed much angrier by the end of the story. "...And so it's all Vanessa's fault!" she finished.

"What did Mr. Mandell even say?" Chelsea asked, taking a delicate bite of pizza.

"He was like, 'I am very disappointed that you would think it's alright to cheat like this. We've talked all about peer pressure, and it seems as if you have been a victim.' And then he went on about pressure and doing the right thing and how bad actions lead to bad consequences and stuff like that. Mr. Mandell said that getting a zero on an important final was enough of a punishment for me."

"So you only get a bad grade?" Adrienne said.

"That's nothing."

"No, it is something, thank you very much. It's a really bad grade. It's the worst possible grade because not only is it an F, it's a ZERO! And it's a zero just because of what Vanessa bullied me into doing."

"Strong words, Quinn. I suggest you watch the way you speak to me," I snapped back.

"And I suggest you watch the way you treat me!"

"And I suggest you two shut up and apologize!" Chelsea yelled.

I gasped. *How dare she!*

"Careful there, Chelsea... Queen Vanessa Pocker might kick you out of the country for giving us a bit of good advice—" Quinn began.

"That means you too, Quinn," Adrienne shot Quinn a warning look.

Chelsea's eyes shifted from me to Quinn. "V. I think you're the one who should apologize first."

I opened my mouth to argue, but Adrienne cut me off. "I think she's right."

I held my tongue for a minute, considering the situation. I needed to keep Quinn around to make Katie jealous, so I couldn't risk any more arguing. The last thing I needed was more drama between the Divas. Even though I didn't really feel sorry, I still mumbled an apology.

"Louder!" Chelsea ordered.

"Sorry, okay?!" I said, a little louder than necessary. *"Sorry!"*

Adrienne looked at Quinn. "You were kind of rude also. Plus, it's not all Vanessa's fault. You're the one who gave in and cheated."

Quinn sighed, and then gave a small smile. "I'm sorry, V. Hug?"

My own lips curved into a small smile also, as my anger started to melt. "Okay." We hugged.

"Okay, now Chelsea and I need to tell you what happened during Science!" Adrienne giggled.

It was all back to normal. For the moment.

Chapter Twelve

I decided to make Sunday a Spa Day. I woke up at eight in the morning and had a lemon poppyseed scone and mint tea. Then, after jumping in the shower to wash my hair, I went upstairs to our family's Spa Room and relaxed in a warm, lavender-scented bubble bath. After soaking in the bubbles for a while, I dried off and threw on a light-pink fluffy bathrobe and matching pompom slippers. I opened the cabinet, pulled out my NARS mud mask, and gently smeared it on. I lay on my back in the spa chair, closed my eyes, and relaxed.

I must have dozed off, because I was awoken by the sound of the doorbell. "Mom, the doorbell!" I shouted. No reply. "Mom! The door!" Still no answer. "MOM!" Nothing. "Ugh!" I huffed, reluctantly getting out of my chair and heading downstairs. *Mom is probably still getting her precious beauty sleep,* I thought angrily. I looked through the peephole. *Quinn*. I swung the door open. "What are you doing here, Quinn?"

"Ohmigod, V, it's a fashion *emergency*!" Quinn said. "You *have* to help me! … Er…. can I come in?"

I stepped aside. Quinn rushed in. I shut the door behind her and led the way to the living room. We sat down.

"Okay, what's the problem?" I asked.

"Well, I got a last-minute invite to my cousin's birthday party," Quinn began, fidgeting nervously. "And I have nothing to wear, and the party's tonight," she said. Her voice rose a little bit when she added, "And he has really cute friends!"

"Okay, calm down," I said. "I'm here for you. You'll be totally fine. Now, is the party going to be at his house, or…?"

"Yes, it's going to be at his house, in the backyard. Nobody's allowed inside," Quinn said nervously.

"Mmhmmmmm," I said slowly, thinking. "And his friends are *cute*?"

"Yeah. And they're about our age. So it's not like they're sixteen or anything."

"Okay. So you'll need something that looks cool. Are your parents going to be there?"

"No. Neither are my uncle and aunt."

"Okay…" I began to daydream, considering the tempting possibilities of an unsupervised party full of hot guys…

"Um, Vanessa?" Quinn said. I snapped out of it and looked at her to show that I was listening. "Do you mind, uh, going shopping with me? So that we can find the perfect outfit? My mom is waiting outside in the car. She can drop us off."

"Oh. Yeah, yeah, of course," I said, rolling my eyes. "Everyone always wants the expert to come along. It's okay, I'll go with you. Let me just clean up and change, and leave a note for Mom."

I dashed into my bathroom, where I washed the mud mask off my face and brushed my hair into a low ponytail. Then I quickly scribbled a note and threw on a blue Juicy scoopneck top and grey True Religion jeans. I grabbed my purse, slipped on my black Steve Madden flats, slapped the note on the kitchen table, and headed for the door.

☆ ☆ ☆

"First stop, Betsey Johnson!" I announced gleefully.

"Why do you love Betsey Johnson so much?" Quinn said.

"Because everyone knows that Betsey Johnson is the *best*," I snapped, taking Quinn by the arm and dragging her into the store. "And, um, *I'm* the fashion expert, not you. So I know exactly what you need."

"But I thought I wasn't a designer girl —"

"You're *not*, okay?! But this is a special occasion so it calls for a special outfit! Do you want to impress some guys or not?" I hissed.

Quinn opened her mouth to say something, but changed her mind and closed it again.

"I'll pay, okay?" I added. "You just keep the clothes. They will come in handy for times like this."

Quinn followed me to a rack of pants. I pulled out a pair of faux leather leggings. Quinn stared at them, wordlessly. Then I went over to the shirts and picked up an oversized black and silver striped t- shirt with the word "Rocker" scrawled across the center. It had torn up sleeves. I knew the guys at the party would love it. "On second thought, I'll keep this shirt after the party," I said.

"Vanessa, um, that shirt is very... erm... *provocative*." Quinn managed, awkwardly.

"Well, too bad. You're wearing it anyway. Wear another shirt under it, if you *have* to. Is it the torn up sleeves that you don't like?"

"That, and the length of the shirt..."

"Oh *please*, it only shows a little belly." I rolled my eyes. Quinn was so lame sometimes. Thank goodness she had me.

Quinn rubbed her forehead and shrugged. "Okay, fine, Vanessa. I'll wear it..."

I smiled triumphantly.

After shopping, Quinn's mom dropped us back off my house. "I'll just wait in the car while you say goodbye to Vanessa," Quinn's mom told her, as we climbed out of her Volvo. "Take your time, girls, we're not in a rush," she added.

"Thanks!" Quinn replied, hurrying inside with me.

"Faux leather leggings!" Quinn shouted, as soon as I shut the front door. "*Faux leather leggings*, and an... um... *revealing*... top! Do you really think this outfit's a good idea, Vanessa?!"

"Yes. I do. You were talking about his cute friends, and if you want them to like you, you're going to have to look hot. And for real, Quinn, that top is not that revealing..."

"Well it's not age-appropriate, I can tell you that!"

"Oh my gosh, Quinn, who honestly cares? '*Age-appropriate?*' You sound like a grandma!"

"I care!" Quinn shouted.

"Then wear a freaking shirt under it! You just have to look cool, okay?" I exhaled. "You are so annoying!" For a minute, we just stood there awkwardly. I stared at Quinn. She stared at the floor. Finally, I decided to break the silence. "You have flats at home, right?" I asked.

"I have black, white, and hot pink—" Quinn replied shakily.

"Hot pink. Perfect. Wear those tonight," I ordered. "And for your makeup..." I sighed. "No eyeshadow. Just mascara, black eyeliner, pink lips."

"That's so not *me*, Vanessa!" Quinn protested.

"I. Don't. Care."

"Isn't it important to be true to who you are? I don't want one of those boys to like me for who I'm not—" she began.

"You know what, Quinn? Every single guy that I have ever had a crush on thought I was hot, so when it comes to guys, don't think I'm wrong. Do you want them to think that you're hot?"

"Um... yes."

"Then take my tips, because if I were you, I'd do the same thing, and everyone thinks I'm beautiful! Do you understand?"

"Yes..."

"Good. Now leave. Have fun. Video chat with me tomorrow and tell me how everything went." I was so frustrated with how difficult she was being.

"Okay, bye. Thanks, I guess…" Quinn muttered, closing the door behind her.

✪ ✪ ✪

The next morning, the strangest thing happened. Around ten in the morning, I got an invitation to video chat from Quinn. I clicked "accept" excitedly. I was expecting her to thank me and compliment my genius.

"Vanessa, I am so mad at you!" she exclaimed.

"Why?"

"Because of that stupid outfit you made me wear! Not only was it uncomfortable, but Adam's friends looked at me all weird! I felt so awkward! And I have rashes on my legs, thanks to those leggings! *And it's all your fault!*" she sobbed hysterically.

"Take a chill pill, Quinn," I said. "I'm sorry, okay? Jeez."

"That's a lame apology," she snapped.

My eyes widened. "Hey, Quinn, you have no permission to talk to me like that."

Quinn looked away.

"I'm sorry, Quinn."

Quinn left the video chat without another word.

What had I done?

I immediately called Ryan.

"Hey Vanes—" he began.

"Ryan! Quinn can't wear shorts anymore thanks to me!" I cut in.

"Uh, what?"

I explained the whole story, starting from Quinn desperately ringing my doorbell to Quinn leaving the video chat without a goodbye. "I ruined everything!"

"Vanessa, it's okay! Did you try apologizing?"

"Yes!"

"And Quinn didn't accept it?"

"She didn't!"

"Did you say 'sorry' sincerely?"

"Yes, I did!"

Ryan gasped softly. "And she still didn't accept it? Oh my gosh. You *never* apologize sincerely!"

"Exactly! She's really mad! I don't know what to do!" I panicked.

Ryan hushed me. "Relax, V. Just go with the flow! I'm sure that Quinn will forget about it by tomorrow, 'kay?"

I sighed. "If you say so..."

"V? I'd love to stay and chat, but I have to run to the grocery store with my mom. Bye!"

"Bye, Ryan." I hung up and collapsed on my bed.

Chapter Thirteen

The next day, the Sassy Divas went out for ice cream after school. Ryan was right. Quinn had seemed to put the argument behind her. Everything seemed pretty normal, until we ordered our ice cream.

After we were served, Quinn pulled me aside. "Vanessa, can I talk to you alone?" she whispered.

"Sure," I replied. "Chelsea, Adrienne, go get a table. We'll join you in a second." The other two girls headed to our usual cozy spot by the window.

Quinn waited for them to get too far away to hear, before quietly leaning in towards me. "I want to quit."

"Quit?" I repeated the word, confused. *Quit what?*

"I want to quit the Sassy Divas," Quinn looked me apologetically.

I laughed nervously. "Very funny, Quinn, but please don't joke about that."

"I'm not joking. I want to quit. I had a lot of fun with you guys, though. Thanks so much for the makeover, and for all the new clothes."

"Ohmygosh, this is all Katie's fault!" I exclaimed.

"No, it's not!" Quinn replied.

My whole world was shattering. *First Katie, now Quinn? Was everyone going insane?*

"Thanks for the ice cream, V—" Quinn interrupted my thoughts. She looked down at her chocolate chip double-scoop, which was starting to melt.

"Don't call me V," I said sternly, my voice shaking. "That's what my *friends* call me."

"Listen, Vanessa, I'm really sorr—"

"NO. Leave. Don't talk to me ever again."

Quinn took a few steps, then hesitated, looking back at me. My arms were crossed. I raised my eyebrows, glaring at her furiously. "Um... guess I'll see you around, Vanessa," she murmured quietly.

I didn't reply.

Once she was gone, I looked over at our table to find Adrienne and Chelsea gaping at me. "Yeah, she's gone!" I said loudly. "And I want you guys to treat her *worse* than you treat Katie. Got it?"

"Got it," they chorused.

As I walked over to my Divas, I texted Ryan:

I HATE QUINN.

Ryan texted back: **What happened now?!**

"One second," I mumbled to my Divas, placing my cup of mint ice cream on the table next to Chelsea. I walked out of the store and called Ryan, like I always did when I needed to talk to someone.

"Vanessa, what's wrong now? Why do you hate Quinn all of a sudden?" he asked.

"I did *everything* for her, Ryan. I made her a part of The Sassy Divas, I gave her an expensive makeover, we hung out, we had fun, I bought her so many things, I helped her with all her fashion problems and now she just leaves me!" I spat.

"I'm sure she left for a reason," Ryan simply stated.

My eyes grew wide. "What's that supposed to mean?"

"It's pretty self-explanatory. I'm sure she left for a reason," he repeated.

"And what exactly do you think her reason was?"

"Maybe it was because you were being a little controlling?"

"*Controlling?*" I echoed. "What makes you think that?"

"Vanessa.... you can be sort of bossy sometimes. It's no secret. Everybody knows."

"Oh my gosh!" I exclaimed indignantly. "You. Are such. A jerk."

"How am I a jerk?! I'm only being honest!" "I am *not* controlling. Just ask Adrienne and Chelsea! They spend the most time with me, after all."

"Maybe so much time that they've just gotten used to it, wouldn't you say?"

I gasped. "How dare you! I am so generous! I always give people lots of things! I have spent so much money on my friends!"

"Vanessa, Adrienne and Chelsea are like your pretty little robots. They obey you and do everything the way you like it. Your gifts and the instant popularity that comes along with being your friend are what fuels them. Are you telling me you haven't noticed that yet? Are you honestly that crazy to think that you are so wonderful to the point that your 'Sassy Divas' will do anything you say, without some kind of reward? I'm honestly glad I'm a guy, otherwise you would have tried to make me into one of your little robots a long time ago."

I was momentarily speechless. *How long had he been keeping all of this inside of him?* "You are wrong!" I spat. "Adrienne and Chelsea *love* me! You're just jealous because I spend most of my time with them! And, guess what, Ryan? I hate you too!" I ended the call without saying another word.

I didn't need Ryan either.

Chapter Fourteen

The next day at school, Katie, Quinn, and Florence were acting as if they had been friends since the third grade. Katie was like, *Oh, Quinn, I love your outfit today!* and Quinn was like, *Oh, thank you, Katie! I love your shoes!*, even when her shoes were actually *atrocious*. Anybody could see that. My Sassy Divas and I walked past them in the morning and I was like, "Nice shoes, Grandma!" Quinn immediately defended Katie.

"Katie's shoes are super cute!" Quinn said. "Very geek-chic!"

"Oh, please," I said, rolling my eyes. "Geek- chic is so out."

"Since when?"

"Since today!"

"Then what's in?"

"Feather earrings!" I yelled, pointing to the green and blue feathers hanging from Chelsea's ears. "But that trend will probably die quickly *also!*"

"Ugh, those are too flashy," Florence said, rolling her eyes.

"Just ignore her, Quinny," Katie told Quinn.

"Quinny?" I repeated. I laughed, along with the Sassy Divas. "See you later, Quinny, Katie-poo, and Baby Flo!" We walked away laughing loudly.

I thought I overheard Katie mutter something that sounded like, "We'll show her!" but I couldn't be sure.

☆ ☆ ☆

The next day at school, there was a small crowd around Quinn, Katie, and Florence. Everyone was talking about their outfits. *Matching outfits.* I squished through the thick crowd with my Divas. My mouth dropped immediately. So did Adrienne and Chelsea's. Katie, Quinn, and Florence were wearing lime green hoodies, denim shorts, neon green converse with black laces, I HEART DINOSAURS knee-high socks, I HEART DINOSAURS pins, and black nerd glasses. They looked hilarious. My Sassy Divas and I looked so much better in our designer clothes, but for some weird reason, our classmates didn't seem to think so. They were all like, "Oh, you three look so cute!"

Then some girl with *real* glasses yelled, "Quinn, I *knew* you'd be better off without Vanessa!"

"Oh, so *you're* CuddleBunny64!" I shouted angrily, remembering the username of the person who posted that online. She didn't seem to hear me. In fact, nobody seemed to even notice me or the Sassy Divas, which was *horrible*. After a few minutes, I lost it.

"HEY!" I shouted as loudly as I could. Everybody went silent when they heard me yell. I walked to the inside of the circle, where Katie, Quinn, and Flo were, and pushed them aside. The Sassy Divas waited on the edge with the rest of the crowd. They looked pretty surprised. "Hi, I'm Vanessa! Do you guys remember me? *I'm* the Queen of the School!" My voice shook. "What's the big deal with *their* outfits? I could wear the same exact thing! Anybody can go to the mall and buy some I HEART DINOSAURS pins! What's so cool about that?" I heard voices whispering. That was a good sign. "I mean, just *look* at those three idiots!" I laughed. The Sassy Divas laughed with me.

Then I realized that nobody else was laughing with us. I looked around, hesitantly. The crowd looked angry. "Go away!" CuddleBunny64 yelled. "Nobody cares about you *or* your 'Sassy Divas' anymore!" The crowd continued talking. I froze.

Quinn walked up next to me and whispered in my ear, "Vanessa, I think you need to leave the circle."

I trudged back over to my Sassy Divas. I felt completely empty. "Girls?" I said quietly.

"Yeah, Vanessa?" Chelsea whispered back.

I glanced at Adrienne. She was still gaping at Quinn, Florence, and Katie. I snapped my fingers in her face to get her attention. I looked into Adrienne and Chelsea's eyes. "We're going to war." I whispered fiercely.

Chapter Fifteen

"V, everyone is talking about Katie, Quinn, and Flo!" Chelsea whined after school. We were grabbing our things from our lockers.

"It's only because of their stupid outfits!" I said, stuffing my math textbook into my backpack.

"Their outfits were *beyond* stupid!" Adrienne said as she checked her hair in her locker mirror.

"I know!" I agreed.

"I know also," Chelsea said. "But nobody has been talking about us! It's almost like we don't even exist anymore!"

"Chelsea!" Adrienne gasped.

"And everyone's asking them for fashion tips!" Chelsea continued. "I mean, aren't we—"

"Ohmygosh, I'm having a total brainstorm!" I interrupted excitedly. The Sassy Divas looked at me eagerly. "So everyone likes dinosaurs now, right?"

"Yeah..." Adrienne said, curiously.

"Everyone's getting I LOVE DINOSAURS pins, thanks to *them!*" Chelsea complained. Adrienne glared at her. Chelsea sighed. "Yes, everyone likes dinosaurs now. Actually, according to the pins, they pretty much *love* dinosaurs…"

"Chelsea!" Adrienne snapped.

"Thank you, Adrienne," I said. "Anyway, think of it this way. Dinosaurs are a new trend. I mean, I know we *set* trends, but, dare I say it, our status is at risk —"

Adrienne gasped.

"That's what I'm trying to say!" Chelsea whined.

I rolled my eyes, continuing, "So, since our status is at risk, we have to follow certain trends rather than veto them. Do I make myself clear?"

"Yeah," Adrienne said.

"So, we'll be following this trend. Girls, after school we're going to the nearest costume store!" I grinned.

☆ ☆ ☆

After school we went to Kiki's Costumes. It was possibly the best costume store ever. It was huge, and it had all kinds of wigs, costume makeup, accessories, and costumes. Plus, it was open all year, not just for Halloween.

"Ooh, I love it here," Chelsea smiled as she looked around. Her eyes widened when she saw the wigs. "Ohmygosh, is that a hot new celebrity style?" she reached excitedly for a dark purple wig.

"Chelsea!" Adrienne spat, slapping her hand away. "Concentrate!"

"Vanessa hasn't even told us what we're looking for!" Chelsea complained, rubbing her hand.

"We're looking for dinosaur costumes," I said.

Adrienne and Chelsea's mouths dropped open. "We're dressing up as dinosaurs?" Chelsea asked.

"Great idea!" Adrienne waved her hands excitedly.

I walked over to the cashier. "Hi," I smiled. "We're looking for dinosaur costumes?"

"Dinosaur costumes?" he echoed in surprise. He stared at us for a minute. Decked out in our designer outfits, we did not look at all like the type of girls who would normally dress up as dinosaurs. "Okay..." He took us over to the section where the animal costumes were. "This is the best one..." he said, as he pulled out a T-Rex costume that came with a dinosaur snout and everything.

"Or, if you want, you can get a dinosaur mask in the mask section. They're pretty realistic. For toddlers and young kids, we have a brontosaurus... but I don't think you'll be able to fit into the brontosaurus costume..." his voice trailed off.

"We'll go with the T-Rex," I said quickly.

"Cool... if you need any help, just call out my name..." the cashier said. He pointed to his name tag. "I'm Phil..."

"Okay, great," I fake smiled. Phil walked away. I turned to my Divas. "We'll stick with the one with the plastic snout." I handed Adrienne and Chelsea their costumes. I glanced around. "Okay, follow me to the fitting rooms."

After trying on the costumes to make sure that they would fit, we rented them. I mean, we weren't gonna *buy* them. *Gross!* I didn't care if even celebrities ended up buying dinosaur costumes; I would still never buy one. "Okay, girls," I said as we walked out of the store. "Tomorrow, bring a change of clothes just in case, but wear your dinosaur costume to school. And for your makeup... stick with just browns and neutral colors. Chelsea, you can use your green eyeliner. But not the sparkly one. Dinosaurs aren't sparkly."

Adrienne and Chelsea nodded, and we walked home happily. Things were going to get better, I could just feel it.

☆ ☆ ☆

The next morning, I entered school through the back gate, and tried my best not to be seen. I decided to hide in the girls' restroom until the bell rang. Surprisingly, I found Adrienne and Chelsea in there also, dressed in their dinosaur costumes. Their snouts were hanging around their necks on the attached elastic bands. They looked relieved to see me.

"Oh, it's you!" Adrienne breathed a sigh of relief.

"We wanted to wait for you so that we didn't have to go out alone," Chelsea said.

The bell rang. I yanked my snout up and over my nose. "Okay, well I'm here, so let's go."

We walked out the restroom confidently. People stared and whispered. We stopped in the center of the school and posed, waiting for the crowd to surround us. They just kept staring.

"Um... Vanessa?" CuddleBunny64 approached me slowly. "You look so stupid." Everyone in the crowd started laughing, except for us. We kept on posing. I blinked.

"Vanessaur!" someone chanted. "Rawr, rawr, rawr! And there's Adrienne-saur and Chelsea- saurus!"

More laughing.

"Vanessaur is a dinosaur from our imagination!" a girl sang to the tune of the Barney theme song.

Even more laughing.

CuddlyBunny64 took out her cell phone and snapped a picture. "This is so totally going online," she giggled.

I fought back tears of embarrassment. "Let's go, girls," I said. We walked to our lockers, took out our extra clothes, and hurried to the bathroom to change.

✿ ✿ ✿

The rest of the day was a nightmare. Each minute dragged by painfully. I had never been so relieved to hear the bell ring. When I finally got home, I focused on brainstorming about what I could do to get attention (the good kind). After a few hours of soaking in the spa and thinking, I got the perfect idea: crazy colored makeup. I threw on my favorite pink robe, rushed to my room and went online. Of course, Adrienne and Chelsea were already online. I started a chat with them.

VANESSA: Girls!
ADRIENNE: Hey V!
CHELSEA: Hi
VANESSA: I have an idea. So we need 2 get attention, right?

ADRIENNE: The good kind of attention.
VANESSA: Yeah. So, tomorrow we will wear

CHELSEA: What will we wear?

ADRIENNE: She's getting there, Chelsea!

VANESSA: Tomorrow our theme will be... CRAZY COLORED MAKEUP!

ADRIENNE: Great idea!!

CHELSEA: Agreed!

VANESSA: Glad U agree. Plan your makeup 2night, girls! Bye!

ADRIENNE: Bye, V! I'll get planning right away. Bye Chelsea!

CHELSEA: Bye guys! I will also start planning. Good thing I have practically every color of sparkly eyeliner!

ADRIENNE: Your current obsession...

CHELSEA: Yes it is! Bye!

I logged off, feeling satisfied.

I woke up early in the morning. It was going to be a big day. I put on a cute floral-print Betsey Johnson tank top and a pair of J Brand royal-blue skinny jeans. In the bathroom, I carefully lined my eyes with bright blue eyeliner. Then I applied neon green and purple eyeshadow to match the flowers on my tank top. I applied bubblegum-pink lipstick and dark brown mascara. For the finishing touch, I reached into my dresser drawer and took out a pink clip-in hair color streak and clipped it in, just as my mom walked by the open door to my room. She took a few steps back and looked at me questioningly. I turned to look at her. She widened her eyes.

"Honey, what is up with your makeup?" she asked softly. "...Sweetheart, you look... you look so funny!"

"I know," I said.

She approached me and moved a strand of hair out of my eyes. "It's so weird that your school is having another spirit week this year." I had told my mom and dad that I was dressing up because my school was having a second spirit week. Spirit weeks usually happened only once a year, and every day was a special theme, like "Crazy Hair" or "Wear Your School Colors."

"Well, it's true," I said.

"And today is 'Crazy Color Day?'"

"Yup, you guessed it," I nodded. "Anyway, Mom, I have to go to school. Bye."

"Bye, Hon. Have a great day."

When I got to school, I did the same thing as the day before. I slipped through the back gate and into the restroom. After waiting for a couple of minutes, Adrienne and Chelsea showed up. They usually walked to school together because they lived on the same street. Adrienne was wearing a blue and white striped dress by Betsey Johnson. She had neon pink and neon yellow eyeshadow on, and her lashes were coated with dark purple mascara, which was probably Chelsea's. She had bubblegum-pink lipgloss on, just like me. Chelsea was wearing a black tank top and a skirt by Betsey Johnson that was covered in patchwork and ruffles. She wore blue and pink eyeshadow, and her eyes were lined with sparkly dark purple eyeliner. She had black mascara on her lashes and her lips were the same shade as ours, bubblegum-pink and glossy. *Perfect!*

"Oh, girls," I grinned. "We could just join a circus. A circus-themed fashion show!" The Sassy Divas laughed. We walked out of the restroom confidently, just like the day before. Sadly, this time, we got even more weird looks, laughter, and even booing.

"So now it looks like they want to join the circus," CuddleBunny64 laughed.

"Yeah," a girl giggled.

"Guys, just give it up," a boy said, rolling his eyes. I walked straight up to him and glared.

"Give up what?" I demanded.

"You're still trying to be the center of attention," he said. "Obviously."

"Shut up!" I said.

Kids continued to boo at us. The booing got louder. I looked around in horror. *They had the guts to boo me?* I straightened up. "Listen up, you losers. I'm Vanessa Pocker, so you better not get rude with *me*. Got it?"

"CLOWN!" some girl yelled. Everyone laughed.

"SHUT UP!" I yelled. Nobody listened. They all just kept laughing. I stormed away. My Sassy Divas followed me in a hurry.

I don't know how I survived the rest of the school day. I was practically in a daze. Just when I had thought things couldn't get any worse, they had! As soon as I got home, I went online to catch up on the latest school gossip. The first thing that I saw was CuddleBunny64's post: a picture of the Sassy Divas in dinosaur costumes. It had been re-shared thirteen times. I read a few posts.

OMG, today the Sassy Divas were seen looking ridiculous. They looked like clowns!!!

Check out my blog for pictures and a video of the Sassy Divas in dinosaur costumes! Vanessaur, Adrienne-saur, and Chelsea-saurus. My three favorite dinosaurs.

You guys can see Vanessa and her clique at Cirque Du Soleil! Hurry up, the tickets are selling fast!

I had totally made a fool out of myself! Anxious to know more about what people were saying, I forced myself to read another traumatizing post.

"Like" this if you think Vanessa has officially lost her throne.

Liked 46 times?! So many people had liked that post. It was horrible. There was no way I had lost my throne! It was impossible. The last post I read said:

Vanessa can just kiss her throne goodbye. It belongs to Katie, Flo, and Quinn now. I mean, after what Vanessa did today, she cannot rule the school. Can you believe she would actually try to prove to us that she needs to keep her throne by dressing up like an idiot?

By then, I decided that I must be having a nightmare. I pinched myself several times on the shoulder, but nothing happened. I just got pinch marks. *Great, now I couldn't even wear a tank top the next day.* Panicking, I immediately messaged Adrienne and Chelsea.

VANESSA: Girls!

ADRIENNE: Yes, V?

CHELSEA: What's up?

VANESSA: Um, have U seen what the other students are saying online lately?

ADRIENNE: No, let me check.

CHELSEA: Same.

ADRIENNE: OHMYGOSH!

CHELSEA: They're saying U lost your throne!

VANESSA: I know, Chelsea, that's why I told U to check!

CHELSEA: Ohmygosh, what R we gonna do?!

VANESSA: I say we try one last time. We need to do something that will really get their attention.

CHELSEA: We can dress like… Lady Gaga? Haha. Just kidding.

VANESSA: Perfect.

ADRIENNE: Huh?

CHELSEA: OMG, V. R U for real?!

VANESSA: We need 2 dress up like Lady Gaga.

ADRIENNE: V, R U sure this is a good idea?

VANESSA: Of course.

ADRIENNE: Okay, so I know we don't care about school and all, but I really don't want to get suspended or anything 4 wearing revealing clothing!

CHELSEA: We don't have 2 wear the revealing ones.

VANESSA: Or we can make our own. I'll B making a bubble dress. I have 2 start early.

ADRIENNE: I'd rather buy the costumes from Kiki's Costumes, which happens 2 B the perfect place 2 go cuz they have WIGS! A lot of wigs!

VANESSA: Okay. U 2 need to tell your parents U have plans over the weekend!

CHELSEA: Saturday?

ADRIENNE: Saturday's good.

VANESSA: Saturday it is. Hey, U guys can even stay 4 dinner that day.

ADRIENNE: Aww, thanks V!

VANESSA: No prob! C U guys 2morrow!

ADRIENNE: Bye!

CHELSEA: Bye, V! Oh, do U want us 2 do anything special with our outfits, makeup, and/or accessories 2morrow when we get ready 4 school?

VANESSA: Hmm... hippie hairstyle! Have a thin band around your head. It's in style, trust me. I keep on seeing it all over the web.

CHELSEA: Okay, cool! Bye!

ADRIENNE: Bye!

I logged off happily. I was filled with good ideas.

The next day at school, everybody called us the Dinosaur Clowns instead of the Sassy Divas. It was terrible thinking that they weren't intimidated by me when I sashayed through the halls with my Divas. They would just whisper and giggle, "There goes the leader of the Dinosaur Clowns. Careful, if you make her angry, she'll roar." I ignored it though, because I knew we would leave them speechless with our Lady Gaga costumes.

✿ ✿ ✿

On Saturday, Adrienne and Chelsea showed up at around 2:00 p.m., just in time for lunch. We shared a thin-crust Hawaiian pizza and gourmet salad. It was delicious. Then we started discussing our Lady Gaga costumes. "So I have the perfect idea," I announced. "Sunday night, you guys better go to bed early, because on Monday, you guys need to be at my house at, like, 6:00 a.m."

Chelsea's eyes widened. So did Adrienne's. I ignored them.

"So I already started working on my bubble dress. It's so hard to make! I need my mom to sew acrylic bubble ornaments onto a nude colored leotard!"

"Wow," Adrienne said.

"And I found the perfect costumes for you guys at Kiki's. Adrienne. You'll be wearing her costume that's called the 'Silver Sequin Dress.' It's that dress with that big triangle thing on it. And it comes with a cool silver eye mask. We'll accessorize your costume with fishnet stockings, black heels or boots, and a curly bobbed blonde wig."

"Cool!" Adrienne grinned.

"Chelsea. You will be wearing the same outfit as Adrienne, but it's black, not silver. You get fishnets and black heels or boots like Adrienne, but your wig is long, blonde, and has bangs. Your eye mask is black and silver."

"Awesome!" Chelsea smiled.

I smiled back. "And now *my* costume. As you guys know, I will be wearing Gaga's famous bubble dress. My accessories will be plastic heels, fishnets, and a blonde bobbed wig with bangs. It's amazing, and I'm sure I'll look great in it."

"You look great no matter what you wear," Adrienne smiled.

"I know," I grinned. I clapped my hands together. "We're going to start off by finishing *my* outfit. Then we can go to Kiki's Costumes and get everything else. We also need to return our dinosaur costumes."

After finishing my costume (which ended up looking fantastic), we headed over to Kiki's Costumes. Unfortunately, Phil was working again that day. "Oh, hey guys," he said when we entered. "Back again?"

"Yeah," Chelsea muttered, checking her nails.

I handed Phil our dinosaur costumes. "There."

"Thanks..." he mumbled. "So you, uh, you really like costumes, huh?"

I ignored him. The Sassy Divas and I walked over to the wig section. That made Chelsea really happy. She loved wigs.

"Wigs!" she squealed. It wasn't like she wore them regularly, but she was always way too excited about getting some new, bright-colored wig every year for Halloween.

"You guys can rent your wigs if you want. I'm gonna buy mine, just in case I need it for the future."

"You know me..." Chelsea giggled, eagerly eyeing a row of colorful neon wigs.

Adrienne shrugged. "I guess I'll buy mine too. I mean, they're human hair wigs... right?" Chelsea and I nodded. "Okay," Adrienne decided. "Then, yeah, I'll buy one, since I could wear it to school or for a party or something, since it's human hair and all."

"Ooh! Ooh! That's the wig I need, right?" Chelsea asked, pointing at a long light blonde wig with bangs.

"Yup," I replied distractedly, scanning the wig selection. "Ah-ha! There's mine!"

"And that one over there is mine!" Adrienne grinned, pointing to a shimmering blonde bob.

A young lady in her mid-twenties suddenly walked towards us. "Oh, I'm sorry..." she exclaimed, slipping behind the long, wooden wig counter. "I didn't know someone was here! May I help you?"

"Yeah, we need to buy some wigs." I gave her a long look. She wasn't very fashionable, but she was better than Phil, at least.

"Okay!" she replied. "What exactly were you girls looking for?"

"We're all dressing up as Lady Gaga," Adrienne announced.

"We need that long blonde wig with bangs you have over there, a curly bobbed blonde wig, and a bobbed blonde wig with bangs," I said, pointing out each wig with my perfectly manicured fingernails.

"Okay..." the salesgirl responded. She pulled out the wigs we needed and gave them to us. They were each encased in a clear, plastic bag like the ones that store-bought Halloween costumes come in. "There you go! Each wig will be fifty dollars." We swiped our cards with happy smiles.

After purchasing everything, we speed- walked back to my house to find my mom watching another episode of *My Strange Addiction*. She turned her head to smile at us as we entered the house.

"Hi girls! Perfect timing, I just got off the phone with your parents. Adrienne, your parents are coming over for dinner. Chelsea, your parents can't join us, but you're allowed to stay for dinner too. I'll give you a ride home later."

"Yay!" Chelsea smiled.

"Awesome!" Adrienne and I chorused. I turned to my Divas. "You guys wanna go swimming?"

✿ ✿ ✿

Early Monday morning, while my parents were still sleeping, the Sassy Divas knocked on my door. It was around six a.m., but my two Divas looked amazing in their Lady Gaga outfits. Chelsea, who had naturally dark auburn hair and Adrienne, whose natural hair was wavy and light brown, both looked surprisingly great in their blonde wigs. My naturally blonde hair was a very similar shade to my wig, but I looked breathtaking with bobbed hair for a change. We were unstoppable, and I was positive that everyone would love our outfits at school.

Sadly, I was wrong. When we arrived at school, we confidently strutted through the halls, instead of slipping into the restroom like we had done before. I expected a shower of applause and compliments, but instead we received strange looks and some giggles. We stopped and posed.

"Oh my gosh, guys! Three Lady Gaga's just came to our school!" CuddleBunny64 exclaimed loudly and sarcastically, drawing attention. Students started to gather around and laugh.

"What losers!" a boy shouted.

A mini marshmallow hit me on the cheek. *Great.* People were throwing their snacks at us. A potato chip landed next to Chelsea. She smashed it angrily with her chunky black heel. Suddenly, I got really angry too. *People actually had the guts to throw food at us!* I stood with my hands on my hips, trying to look as intimidating as possible. I glared into the crowd in front of me and found Quinn, Katie, and Florence staring at me in shock. *They* weren't laughing, at least.

"Oh, Vanessa looks sooo scary right now!" mocked a girl with a purple streak in her hair, faking a frightened expression. "I think I might pee myself!" More laughing. I stood my ground.

I turned to my Sassy Divas. They were trying to look confident also. I turned back to the crowd, trying my best to tune out their laughter and stupid insults. I stomped my foot. A bubble ornament snapped off of my leotard and shattered on the ground.

"Uh-oh! Somebody's bubble popped!" I heard a girl's voice giggle.

I could feel my face beginning to flush, turning red from the humiliation. I couldn't take it anymore. I quickly pushed my way through the crowd and into the restroom. The Sassy Divas hurried through the path I had cleared, just in time to see me fall to my knees sobbing as the door swung shut behind them. I had lost my throne, and there was nothing I could do about it.

I was such an idiot.

Chapter Sixteen

I stayed in the bathroom for what seemed like hours. Chelsea and Adrienne comforted me for a while, but they eventually had to leave for class. The Sassy Divas had ditched before and they couldn't really afford to miss any more classes this year. I couldn't either, but I didn't care. I had lost my throne, the most important thing to me in the whole world. I couldn't face the rest of the school again, so when I was sure that the hallway was empty, I snuck out of the bathroom. First, I walked slowly, trying to appear calm and normal, in case any school security guards saw me. As I got closer to the wrought-iron back gate, I began walking faster.

Once I made it through the gate, I burst into a full-speed sprint, running down the tree-lined side street like a crazy woman in my ridiculous bubble outfit. Cars were slowing down to gawk at me. I tore off an acrylic bubble and threw it to the ground. It shattered into a million pieces.

When I got home, I ran straight to my room and slammed the door behind me. I tore off what was left of my bubble costume and threw on my comfiest outfit, a lime-green velour Juicy Couture tracksuit. I sat on my bed, wondering what to do. My mind was racing. *If only I knew what all the other kids were thinking.* I didn't feel like reading any more mean, stupid comments from nobodies like CuddleBunny64, but I had to know what was going on. After thinking about it for a while, I finally logged on to my chat account. I guessed that since I wasn't the Queen of the School anymore, I could comment on anybody's posts and they wouldn't care.

But once I started reading people's posts, my heart sunk. *Everybody* was getting I HEART DINOSAURS pins. Some people had even posted pictures of themselves wearing them! Even after everything that had happened, I still wouldn't be caught dead wearing anything dumb like that.

I checked my email and saw an email from Quinn. At first, I thought that maybe it was an old email that I had accidentally missed before, but when I looked at the date on the email, it said it had been sent at four o'clock that afternoon. I looked at the subject. It read:

Forward: Chat Between Katie and I- Please read.

It was a conversation between Quinn and Katie that had been sent to me by Quinn! I immediately began reading.

KATIE: HI QUINN!

QUINN: HI KATIE! What's up?

KATIE: Nothing. You?

QUINN: Same. Listen, I feel really bad about what happened to Vanessa.

KATIE: Why? She's mean to us. She HATES Bookworms.

QUINN: Yeah, but Vanessa's throne meant everything to her.

KATIE: Yeah, I guess.

QUINN: I mean... I kinda miss her. She was fun.

KATIE: So do I.

QUINN: Wait... really?

KATIE: Yeah. She's nice deep down. I KNOW she is. And you're right, she IS fun to be with. I just wish she wasn't so... bossy, and mean, and all that. Plus, I wish she would understand that Bookworms aren't nerds... they just love to read books, and good grades are important to them!

QUINN: Yeah! Nerds do extra credit for fun. I used to be nerdy... maybe we should just talk to Vanessa and her Sassy Divas.

KATIE: Okay, but we need to talk to her alone first.

QUINN: Yup! I have to go now, Katie. See you tomorrow!

KATIE: Bye!

I started to cry. "Untrue! Totally untrue!" I sobbed quietly. But deep down inside, I wondered if some of what they had said might be just a little bit true.

Was I really bossy? Or mean? Was it a crime to just want my friends to be as cool and stylish as I was? I started bawling. Soon, I heard footsteps pounding up the stairs. Someone knocked on my door.

"What?" I snapped.

My mom opened the door. "Sweetheart?"

I sniffled. "What?"

"Is everything alright?"

"Yeah..." I turned away from her and looked out my window, trying hurriedly to wipe my tears away with the sleeve of my velour track jacket. The early evening breeze blew softly. The wind chimes hanging outside my window jingled. My mom sighed. I glanced sideways at her. She sat down on my bed and patted the spot next to her. Reluctantly, I followed her directions and joined her on my blankets.

"Vanessa, I know that something's wrong. Does this have to do with Katie?" she asked softly.

I shrugged.

"Vanessa..." my mom paused, searching for the right words. "I am your mother and I love you no matter what. You should know you can talk to me about anything." She smiled at me encouragingly.

"I dunno..." I began. "It's kinda dumb. It's a problem with Katie, Quinn, me, or all of the above."

"Well, sweetie, maybe talking about it will help you figure this whole thing out. What's wrong with Katie and Quinn?"

"Katie and I split up as friends a long time ago. Then Quinn and I split up as friends too. The two of them started hanging out together, and everyone seems to think that they're cooler than me now!" I huffed. "But I just found out that they both miss me..." my voice trailed off as I finished.

"How did you find that out?" she inquired. I explained about the email that Quinn had forwarded me.

"Okay, and what's going on with you?"

I exhaled. "Well… in the email, they said that they thought I was fun and nice *deep down*."

"Deep down?" she raised her eyebrows.

"Yeah, and they said that they think I've been being a jerk. I'm starting to think that maybe that's why they both stopped hanging out with me."

"In what way were you being a jerk?"

"Apparently, I'm 'bossy, mean, and all that!'" I started tearing up.

"Sweetie, sweetie, sweetie…." my mom shook her head, patting me softly on the back.

"Mom… I think I need your help. I miss Katie and Quinn too, and I want to be friends with them again."

My mom nodded. "Alright, I'll help you. Just remember that ultimately, it's still up to you to solve your own problems."

"Right." I agreed.

My mom took a minute to think about the situation. "Well the only thing you can really do is apologize. Tell them how much they mean to you. Katie and Quinn are sweet girls, and I know that underneath your tough outer shell, you are too."

I rolled my eyes. "Thanks a *lot*, Mom."

"Just being honest. Remember sixth grade?"

"I, uh… I would prefer not to…"

"Just think of it for a second. Tell me how you felt."

I closed my eyes and swallowed. "Well, it felt terrible, obviously."

"Why was it terrible?"

"Because people made fun of me. They made fun of my hair and my skin and my clothes, and my love for books and my good grades."

"Mhmm. And what are you doing to people right now?"

I paused, feeling horrible. It took a while to say it out loud. I started slowly, stuttering. "I'm... making fun of... their looks... and their fashion... and their love for books... and good grades..." My eyes were starting to water again.

"Exactly. Do you remember those times when you cried in the bathroom all night, making faces in the mirror and using my makeup to try make yourself look like a different person?"

I forced back a flood of tears. "Mom, don't bring it up, please..."

"I've noticed your behavior for a while, and I've been meaning to talk to you about it. I think the time is finally right, now that you're finally starting to see how your actions affect those around you. Have you ever thought about how bossy you are? Every day you're snapping at people, saying you don't care about what they think or want, rolling your eyes, and acting superior to everyone else. You don't seem to realize how everyone around you constantly bends over backwards to try to keep you happy. Take some time to think about it. Keep in mind, Vanessa, having friends is a privilege, not a right."

Her words slapped me in the face. Before she could stop me, I stormed out of my room and locked myself in the nearest bathroom. "Vanessa..." my mom pleaded, knocking lightly on the bathroom door. "I didn't mean to upset you... and I know it's tough stuff to hear, but I'm just trying to help you." She waited outside the door for a while, but I didn't respond. I waited for the sound of her footsteps to fade away before letting my sobs out. I buried my face in my hot pink monogrammed bath towel. My initials, "V.P.", were stitched on it in gold thread, beneath an embroidered gold tiara. *Queen Vanessa,* I thought to myself. *Was my throne really so important to me?*

I closed my eyes and sighed, leaning back against the pink and white striped wallpaper. My mom was right. All this time, I had acted as if it was a privilege for the other girls to have a friend like me, when it turned out that I was actually the one who was lucky to have them. Let's face it, Katie was totally innocent and sweet. She was sick of me, which I could understand now. Quinn was the nicest girl I had ever met. I must have been a really bad friend to push away two girls who were such kind people. Adrienne and Chelsea should be the ones with the tiaras, not me. They were truly the Queens of Loyalty. Following me around, listening to me, talking to me, dealing with my constant eye rolls and insults and selfishness. They deserved at least ten Burberry trench coats. *Each.* As for Ryan... he was perfect. He tried to fix me before it was too late, and I instead of listening, I told him I hated him and hung up. He had always been there for me and had always put up with my attitude. I pondered for a few minutes. Suddenly, I had the perfect idea.

"I think I know how to fix this," I smiled, drying my eyes.

I walked out of the bathroom and into my room. I called Ryan, silently pleading that he wouldn't ignore my call.

"Hello? Vanessa?"

"Ryan..." I said. I exhaled. "I am so deeply sorry. You have no idea. I have thought about my actions all evening, and I've settled on this: I suck."

Ryan let out a small laugh.

"No, really. I have been such a gigantic turd. You are so special, Ryan, did you know that? You help me with my problems all the time. I've just now realized that most of my problems were stupid, but guess what? You helped me anyway. And I love you for that. In a friend-way, of course! I mean, you put up with my attitude, and you've tried to help me fix my personality... but I was an idiot and hung up on you. Had I just listened to you, I could've prevented all of this from happening. It might be too late to fix people's opinions about me, but I'm still gonna give it a shot."

There was an awkward silence on his end of the line. I continued. "I really, honestly have thought about everything I've done, and even remembered the bullying I received in the past over my appearance and Bookworm ways... and I remembered how it felt and I've realized that no girl deserves to feel the way I did. I know it's selfish, but I had thought that making fun of other people would make me feel better about myself, but it hasn't really helped at all." I added, hoping that Ryan would make a noise to show that he was listening the whole time.

There was still silence.

"Ryan...?" I asked softly.

"I... I don't know what to say...." Ryan finally managed. "But, to be honest, I'm glad you've finally realized this."

I smiled and nodded, even though he couldn't see me.

"Thanks for calling me special, V," Ryan added, letting out a small laugh.

I laughed too. "Just being honest."

Chapter Seventeen

When I arrived at school the next morning, I was feeling optimistic. I was dressed fantastically in my favorite designer, Betsey Johnson: a black cap-sleeved shirt and my favorite floral skirt. The only thing not Betsey Johnson was my shoes— navy flats by White Mountain Hotcakes. My hair was perfectly flat-ironed, and my accessories were tasteful and carefully chosen. I had spent the whole night planning what to say. I was as ready as I was ever going to be to talk to Katie, Quinn, Adrienne, and Chelsea.

First, I went to Adrienne and Chelsea, thinking it would be easier to start with them. I found them sitting at our usual table.

"Hey girls," I beamed.

"Hey, V," Adrienne replied.

"What's up?" Chelsea asked.

"I just wanted to let you know that I am really sorry about being such a jerk."

Adrienne and Chelsea looked at each other in surprise.

"Are you alright, Vanessa?" Chelsea asked, slowly.

"Yes! Of course! I'm just saying that I realized what I have been doing wrong. So... do you accept my apology?"

Adrienne and Chelsea looked at each other again, then turned back to me, wide-eyed.

"Definitely," Adrienne said. Chelsea nodded, in shocked agreement.

"I'm kinda confused as to what made you suddenly feel this way..." Chelsea mumbled, looking up at me questioningly.

"Oh!" I laughed. "Well, I got a forwarded message from Quinn. It was a chat between her and Katie, and they were talking about me. They said some nice things, but they also said some mean things... that I kinda realized were true... when I got this lecture from my mom. At first I was really mad, but then I thought about it all, and it just made sense. I guess I never really tried to put myself in anyone else's Jimmy Choos before."

"Wow," Chelsea murmured. "That's deep." I smiled at her and Adrienne. They smiled back. "Well, that's cool," Chelsea finished, changing the subject. "Anyway, yesterday I saw the *cutest* top—"

"Sorry guys, I have to go apologize to Katie, Quinn, and Flo too. I'll catch you later!" I waved as I took off.

As I hurried away, I heard Adrienne call out, "By the way, V, nice skirt!" In my head, I didn't even say *I know*. Instead, I said, *Thank you* (even though a tiny part of me knew that it was the cutest skirt ever). My eyes scanned the grass. I found Quinn, Florence, and Kaie sitting in a sunny area on the grass. I walked over to them.

"Hi guys." I began, with a self-assured smile.

"May we help you?" Katie snapped.

"I just wanted to apologize."

Katie looked at Quinn. Quinn stared down at the grass, awkwardly. Florence pretended to skim through the pages of her book.

"For what?" Katie asked.

"For being conceited, bossy, and a jerk, all at once."

The corners of Katie's mouth crept up into the tiniest of smiles. "What made you open your eyes?" Katie asked.

Quinn looked up. She met my eyes and gave the smallest shake of her head, looked to Katie, then back to me. She wanted me to keep the email she had forwarded me a secret. *No problem.*

"My mom gave me a lecture about my behavior. I never really thought about how I was acting before.

She helped me see how selfish and bossy I was being. I'm seriously sorry." I explained to Katie.

"I see..." Katie's smile grew a little wider.

"Will you guys accept my apology?"

Katie looked at Quinn and Florence. "Quinn? Flo?"

"Of course," Quinn smiled.

Flo cracked a smile. "I suppose."

"We can totally be friends, Florence. I'm sorry for putting you on the list of people the Divas aren't allowed to talk to. And, uh... your hair is flawless."

Flo beamed.

"So what do you say, Katie?"

Katie's sparkling emerald eyes beamed up at me. "Yes."

I beamed back at her. "Thank you. And please forgive the Sassy Divas too. They were just trying to please me. They're very nice girls and super loyal."

"I figured," Katie said. "Thanks, um... V."

"Thank you." I grinned. I finally had my best friends back.

Quinn and Katie grinned back at me.

Epilogue

I would be lying if I said that the story ended here, with Katie and Quinn rejoining the Sassy Divas. It didn't. Instead, we joined forces with the Bookworms and renamed our clique the Classy Divas, imparting facts from what we learned in class—dinosaurs being the first topic of knowledge.

Just kidding, that didn't happen either. The Sassy Divas and the Bookworms stayed two different cliques, but we didn't waste time fighting anymore. My friends and I just hung out, having fun and doing what all girlfriends do. Being divas, setting trends, and maybe even reading a book or two…

Meet the Author: Yalda Alexandra Saii

Yalda Alexandra Saii is an avid reader, writer, and a student of Lekha School of Creative Writing, which she has attended since 2009. Her short stories and creative works have been published in numerous anthologies, including *Adventures of the Imagination*, the annual Lekha student anthology. *The Sassy Divas* is her first solo novel. Yalda began writing *The Sassy Divas* during a Lekha class when she was ten years old, and completed it at the age of twelve. Her passion for writing is ever-growing, and she hopes to publish many more books in the future. Currently, Yalda lives with her family in the San Francisco Bay Area.

The Lekha Way

At Lekha, we believe that the ideas of children are rooted more in imagination than those of adults, who tend to think more pragmatically. It is this imagination that the Lekha School of Creative Writing wishes to nurture and develop. By learning how to turn their imagination into words, children learn how to put ideas on paper, thus making them into successful communicators.

As children learn the art of narration, their ideas may not always come across as fluid as one may wish them to, but they are still concrete ideas that can attain perfection with some training. A three- headed cat that turns into tomatoes, a spider defeating a lion, or a mad scientist befriending a computer — these are just a few examples of how the Lekha Way can bring out the imagination of a child.

Lekha Publishers LLC, an independent publishing company, has been conducting after- school classes, enrichment programs, week-long day camps, and workshops for children since 2006, as part of its educational outreach department. For more details about our programs, please visit our website: www.lekhaink.com.

CPSIA information can be obtained at www.ICGtesting.com
Printed in the USA
LVOW131131270313

326317LV00001B/1/P